The Village That Slept

The Village
That Slept

by Monique Peyrouton de Ladebat

Translated from the French by Thelma Niklaus

ILLUSTRATED BY MARGERY GILL

WITH A NEW INTRODUCTION BY
CHARLOTTE A. GALLANT

GREGG PRESS
BOSTON

Text copyright © by Éditions G.P., Paris, 1961. English translation and illustrations © by The Bodley Head Ltd., 1963 Reprinted by arrangement with The Bodley Head Ltd.

Introduction copyright © 1980 by Charlotte A. Gallant

Gregg Press Children's Literature Series logo by Trina Schart Hyman

New material designed by Barbara Anderson

Printed on permanent/durable acid-free paper and bound in the United States of America

Republished in 1980 by Gregg Press, A Division of G.K. Hall & Co., 70 Lincoln St., Boston, Massachusetts 02111

First Printing, January 1980

J

P

Library of Congress Cataloging in Publication Data

Peyrouton de Ladebat, Monique, 1909-
    The village that slept.

    (Gregg Press children's literature series)
    Translation of Le village aux yeux fermés
    Reprint of the 1965 ed. published by Coward-McCann, New York.
    SUMMARY: Two youngsters find themselves stranded with an infant near a deserted village high on a desolate mountain.
    [1. Survival—Fiction. 2. Science—Fiction]
I. Gill, Margery. II. Title. III. Series.
[PZ7.P4482Vi 1979]   [Fic]   79-18363
ISBN 0-8398-2610-9

Introduction

ABOY and a girl, survivors of an unknown accident, find themselves lost on a mountain without any memory of how they came to be there. They discover a tiny baby strapped in his carrying case and add him to their little group. But about themselves they can remember only that their names are Franz and Lydia.

When the children fail to find a path down the mountain, they realize that they will have to take care of themselves and the baby until they are rescued. They find a village but it is deserted. Lydia finds a little house that is snug and homelike; Franz discovers an Alpine hut stocked with provisions, even a few books, and the children begin to settle in. By the time winter comes, they have made themselves secure against the weather and the loneliness.

The Village That Slept (1963) was first published at a time when survival stories were extremely popular. Although this is not a suspense story of overcoming grim disaster, there are enough of the elements of fear and loneliness, inventiveness and ingenuity that the story falls into this category.

There is a certain unreality about the plot because the children cannot remember who they are and what has happened. They do not realize the significance of the red glow in the sky, nor the roar as though something were plunging down the mountainside, nor why they see the glowing embers of a great fire that is just dying out; and so the reader does not immediately understand the significance of these things either.

The formal style of conversation, although it may be the result of translation, tends to heighten this sense of unreality, as does the mystery surrounding the children's identity. Not until the end of the book does the reader know who the children are and how they came to be on the mountain.

The situation presented in the story is improbable, of course, because everything falls into place too easily for the children. The Alpine hut provides food and essentials, and the little house is quickly discovered. "Survival" is idealized and relatively unthreatening and this is part of the charm of the story. The independence of the children, the absence of adults, and the chance to "play house" are themes which appeal to children.

Lydia makes the house cozy with a vase of flowers; Franz builds a bookcase to house their books. Lydia finds blankets which she airs in the sun; Franz chops wood for the fire. Lydia devises a warmer coverlet from two of the blankets; Franz makes a reed pipe to entertain themselves. The children feel a tremendous satisfaction in getting themselves settled, and in making a home after being lost and defenseless.

When a dog, a cow, a sheep, and two chickens wander into the yard several weeks later, the children have new friends and a source of fresh eggs and milk to add to their supplies.

However cozy these arrangements, the children cope with real problems. They feed the baby wet biscuit crumbs, and give him a handkerchief dipped in water to suck. Franz finds a dead animal which he skins to make shoes. They hang a blanket over the door to shut out the cold.

The emphasis is on the sense of security which the children create within their own little home and their feeling of being able to conquer problems; so although winter brings blizzards and snow and confinement, it holds no insurmountable terrors for them.

How the children react to being alone and

how they react to each other is the main focus of the story. Franz and Lydia take courage from the fact that there are two of them. They know that they must rely on each other. The responsibility of a baby to care for makes them realize that they must struggle through for little Tao no matter how discouraged and frightened they feel. They understand that "their hours and days until they are rescued will be exactly what they have the courage to make them" (p. 28).

There are many moments of panic and despair. When Franz is gone terror engulfs Lydia: "Her heart was beating so fast she felt she would suffocate, her hands were frozen, and a cold sweat had broken out on her forehead" (p. 33). It is only the thought that she must not add to Franz' anxiety by showing her own that helps her overcome her frightening sense of despair; and so she washes the baby's clothes.

When Lydia is gone from the house, everything seems dark to Franz, but when she comes back, it is "as if she brought the sun with her" (p. 57).

The words and phrases point up the feelings of despair: "somber," "indefinable cold seeped down," "darkness, frightening, heavy and full of menace," "gloomy clouds writhed down from the mountain peaks," "despair rushed back, blacker than . . . earlier."

And contrasted against the frightening feelings are happier moments: flames that are "friendly and reassuring," the "heartening sound" of Franz' axe, etc. When the children feel safe and secure, the author lets the reader feel safe and secure also.

Finally after a long 18-month ordeal, the children are rescued. The rescue takes place in a perfectly logical manner. The loose ends of the story are tied up in a sensible explanation, the strangeness is gone, the mystery explained, and it becomes perfectly clear why the children were alone on the mountain.

And now that they are being rescued and will have to give up their little family, Franz and Lydia realize how much they have loved their house and their garden, and even the menacing mountain. But Lydia's parents arrange for the animals to go to their country home, Franz' grandfather stays in Paris so the children will not be separated, and little Tao is permitted to stay with Lydia.

In this International Year of the Child, the story has an added significance since Lydia is discovered to be French, Franz is Austrian, and baby Tao is Oriental. But working together they have accomplished a miracle.

When the children are asked what they would like as a reward for rescuing the pilot, who in turn has brought about their own rescue, they ask for the deserted village to become a place for sick children and for children without any parents. Lydia says, "It must be for all kinds of children . . . for we came from three different countries, and we loved each other like brothers and sister. It must be for any lost children in the world" (p. 187).

The ending is idealized and completely satisfying.

Charlotte A. Gallant
Cleveland, Ohio, 1979

The Village That Slept

1

THE GIRL opened her eyes and tried to make out her surroundings. There was nothing but darkness, a warm and
heavy darkness. She was lying uncomfortably on a rocky
slope tufted with coarse grass, and her drowsy mind was
wrapped in a darkness as heavy as that of the night that
enfolded her. She could remember nothing, nothing at all.
Painfully she dragged herself up on both hands from the
pebbles rolling down the slope, and tried to probe her memory, but there was nothing but a gaping hole, empty of all
remembrance. It was as though life had begun for her at
that moment, and she had just opened her eyes for the
first time. She got up and began walking, trying to shake
off the terror that had come on her. There was no path.
She stumbled along over the rubble, through the tough
scrub that scratched her legs. The night was ink black,
without moon or stars. Which way should she go? As
though by instinct she made towards a patch of sky less
dark than the rest; it seemed to be lit by a dim red glow.
She wondered if it could be the rising sun. Behind it great
chaotic masses that must be mountains towered dark

against the dark sky. It was terrifying to be so alone. There was no sound, not even an animal, no dog barking, no bird singing, nothing but this vast silent darkness.

She had no idea how she came to be here, or what had happened; she did not know her own name or what day of the week it was, what month, or what year. She only knew that she had received a heavy blow on the head and that her head was still aching badly. She felt her forehead and ran her hand through her hair, but she found no wound, nor any trace of bleeding.

She stumbled on, tired now, dreadfully tired. She wondered how far she must go, and whether she would ever arrive anywhere. She even wondered if she were dead and walking through limbo. The red glow in the sky ahead of her was fading instead of spreading, so it could not be the rising sun. It seemed that this nightmare would never end. If only it could turn out to be nothing but a bad dream! For a long time she struggled on, not knowing whether she was making progress or simply going around in circles, since there was no landmark to guide her; until at last she sat down on a boulder and burst into tears.

She could not go on wandering around like this. It would be better to wait, for sooner or later day must come, and surely there must be an end to this ordeal. Suddenly she thought she heard a moaning sound, and she stopped weeping to listen. It was not very loud, but quite clear, a moan or a cry for help. She got to her feet, forgetting how tired she was, and ran over the loose rubble and the thorny scrub in the direction of the sound. Almost at once she made out a dark shape stretched upon the ground, and immediately she was afraid it must be a wild animal. She stood still a moment, wondering whether the thing would jump up and attack her. Then the cry came again, urgent and mournful. She summoned all her courage and forced herself to go forward and lean over the dark shape. It was a child, a boy who seemed to be about her own age. He lay there with his eyes closed, and in the darkness his face was unnaturally pale. He was groaning without knowing what he was doing.

She put her hand on the boy's forehead, and he shivered at her touch. Then she knelt beside him and breathed gently on his mouth and eyelids in an effort to bring him around. He opened his eyes.

"Oh, it hurts!" he said, rolling his head on the hard ground.

"What does?"

"My leg."

She felt his legs and found that one of them was covered in something thick and sticky that might be blood.

"Where are we?" he asked.

He tried to lift himself, and she helped him to sit up.

"Where are we?" he said again, looking around.

"I don't know."

"Who are you?"

"I don't know."

"What are you doing here?"

"I don't know."

He drew his hand over his forehead as though he were brushing away a nightmare.

"I'm dreaming."

"I don't think you are."

They looked at each other for a while in a silence heavy with foreboding, trying to see each other in spite of the darkness.

"How did you get here?" she said.

"I don't know."

9

"Does your leg hurt badly?"

"Yes, it does. It hurts an awful lot . . . my leg, I mean. But that doesn't matter, the important thing is to find out —"

"Find out what?"

"Why we're here."

"What's your name?"

"I don't know."

"Oh, I *am* glad I've found you," she said, clasping his hand. "I was so frightened, all by myself. It was awful! But . . ." she added after another silence, "I wish you hadn't hurt your leg."

"I expect it will be all right. Perhaps it'll be better by tomorrow. I wish I knew what's happened."

Once more he looked around.

"It's so dark here; it's very eerie."

"I woke up some time ago," she said. "And I walked and walked and walked. I did so want to find something, or someone. Then I got so tired I sat down and cried. And that's when I heard you."

"I'll try to get up. Maybe if we go on walking, we'll find something."

"Lean on me . . . like this. Can you stand up? Does that hurt? Do you think you can walk?"

"Yes, I think I can, if I lean on you."

"We'll go slowly."

They started walking, the girl helping the boy along. He was taller and sturdier than she, and now that he was on his feet he looked older. She had to stretch up to support him.

"There's a red glow in the sky," he said. "We can go by that."

But as they continued towards it, a roar broke the si-

10

lence, as though something were plunging down the mountainside into the darkness below.

"Look," the girl cried, "the glow is fading away. You can hardly see it any more."

Doggedly they went on, the boy gritting his teeth in an effort to hide the pain of his leg. They walked around a mass of rock towering high above them, and came suddenly upon the glowing embers of a great fire that was just dying down.

"So that's what it was," said the girl, "that red light in the sky."

"What on earth could have made a fire like that?" the boy wondered.

By the light of the fire the girl could see a huddle of houses clinging to the side of the mountain. She pointed towards it. "Look, we shall be safe there."

"I believe you're right. It looks like a village."

"Can you last until then?"

"I don't think I can. Tomorrow, maybe. But I can't go on now. My leg hurts too much, and I'm so tired."

"I'm tired too," she said. "I can't go a step farther."

"Well then, let's lie down by this tree and try to sleep until morning. Tomorrow everything will seem better, and we'll make for the village."

"Yes, you're right," said the girl. "We'll camp in this hollow by the tree-trunk. We'll be fine, the roots make a sort of shelter. Even if the wind blows we won't feel it here."

He took off his coat and spread it on the ground. "There you are, lie on that. There's even moss growing here — it'll make a good pillow!"

"I'll take my coat off too and put it over us for a blanket."

"Will you be comfortable?"

12

"Oh yes, it's almost like being in a real bed. You lie down too, quickly."

The boy curled up in the narrow space in the shelter of the protecting roots, and covered their legs with the girl's coat.

"It's a miracle, finding you like this," she said. "I would have died if I'd been alone in this field — I'd be terrified!"

"Go to sleep now. Everything will be all right tomorrow. There's nothing to be frightened of! I'm here, and I'm strong enough for anything."

"Is your leg hurting very much?"

"No, not really."

He held her hand, and she fell asleep almost at once. In a little while he too was fast asleep, in spite of his aching leg.

2

SHE WAS still sleeping when he woke, roused to consciousness by the pain of his wound that had started throbbing again when he moved his leg suddenly. The sun was well up, and for a moment he was bewildered to find himself in the hollow of a tree, under a clear sky against which the high peaks of hazy blue mountains stood out sharply. Stony fields scattered with brushwood spread here and there among the peaks. The red sun touched the highest mountains while the others lay in velvety shade. The sharp air was intoxicating and so pure it almost took his breath away. An unknown little girl, still fast asleep, rested her head on his shoulder and leaned against him. Her hair gleamed like molten gold against the dark stuff of her dress.

He began to wonder why he was there, and what had happened, but could think of no answer. His mind was blank, empty; he remembered nothing. The only things that came into it were the confusion of the night before, the sudden appearance of the girl — so oddly beside him when he woke up — the pain in his leg, the cruel trek in

14

total darkness over rough ground, and then the feeling of comfort that gradually came over him when they lay down beneath the long roots that sheltered them like outstretched arms. He kept still a long time so as not to wake her, and took a good look at her. She had a straight little nose and her long dark lashes lay upon pale cheeks. There she was, alive and breathing, and he was glad of another living being in the barren silence that seemed to reign in this place.

She must have sensed that someone was looking at her. Her eyelids fluttered, then she opened her eyes. She pushed back her hair and half-lifted her head. "Where are we?" she asked. "Who are you? What are you doing here?"

"That's just what I was thinking about," he said.

She looked all around her, and when she lifted her face to the gilded peaks of the mountains it was as though the weight of her hair dragged her head backwards.

"What country is this? — How high these mountains are! — But what am I doing here — with you, when I don't know you?"

"I've no idea . . . it's like having a big black hole in my head. All I keep seeing is last night, when I woke up with an awful pain in my leg, and you were standing in front of me."

"It's the same with me, only I've still got a headache. Yes, it's just like you said, a big black hole. I woke up in the night, I was very frightened, and I walked on and on, all by myself, and I was crying, until I found you. Something has happened to us, I know, but what is it?"

"What's your name?" he asked her.

She frowned in an effort to remember. "I just don't know," she said. "It's on the tip of my tongue but I can't remember. What's yours?"

15

He too struggled to remember, striving to find some little flash of light in his confused mind. Then suddenly he smiled.

"Yes, I've got it. It's come back to me! I remember! — Franz," he said at last, nearly crying with relief. "Franz, but that's all. I must have another name, but I can't remember, I just can't remember any more."

"I can't remember anything at all," she said.

"There's a locket around your neck. Let me see — look, your name's on it — *Lydia*. And the date you were born, too."

"Lydia," she repeated mechanically. "Lydia . . . Lydia . . . That's right, I remember — Lydia. And I'm twelve, I know I'm twelve. And you must be older; you're taller and bigger than I am."

"I suppose so," he said, as though he were thinking of something else.

"What are we going to do now?"

"We must get away from here," he said.

"Didn't we see a village last night, just before we went to sleep?"

"Yes, I think so. There was a fire, it lit up a slope that seemed to have houses on it."

"Let's go and see," she said, standing up. "I'm hungry."

She put her coat on for the morning air was sharp, and combed her hair with a comb she found in her coat pocket.

"Lend it to me, will you?" said Franz.

She held it out to him, and he combed his hair too.

"We don't want to look like savages when we meet people," she said.

Franz brushed his coat down with his hands and slung it over his shoulder.

"Let's go!"

16

He took her by the hand, as he had done the night before as they settled down to sleep.

The village they had seen in the darkness tumbled down a nearby slope just caught by the sun. The houses were low built, with overhanging roofs, and Franz noticed that there was no smoke rising from the chimneys, even though at this hour the people living in them would certainly be up and about. He suddenly felt anxious, but said nothing.

Lydia stopped and stood still, as though something had caught her attention.

"Listen," she whispered. "There must be an animal nearby."

"An animal?"

"Yes. There's an odd sort of cry."

Franz listened.

"It's not a cry, it's more like a wailing."

"I'm frightened," Lydia said.

"Why? It's only a little animal. It's such a little voice."

"Don't go!" she said, hanging on to his hand.

"But I must, it may be caught in a trap, it sounds as though it's hurt. Please let go. I'll just look and then come back. Wait here."

"No, no. You mustn't leave me. I'll come too."

"I think it's just about here," said Franz in a low voice.

He walked through the undergrowth towards the rock they had come around last night. Lydia followed him without speaking.

"It's difficult to know exactly where it's coming from," he said after a long silence.

"I think it's by that bush."

"Yes, you're right — I can see something moving there."

"Oh Franz, I'm terrified. It may be an animal ready to leap out at you. Do be careful!"

"I'll get a stick," he said.

Lydia remembered a big dry branch near the tree.

"I'll get it for you — I can run, and you can't."

She was off and back in a flash.

"While you were away I looked hard at it. It's moving, and it's an animal with white fur, but I can protect myself with this stick, so don't be scared."

He went towards the bush, taking care to make no noise, and Lydia followed a little way behind.

"Don't come too near," he said. "Let me see what it is first."

The wailing had grown weaker. Then there was a murmur that tailed off into silence.

Franz, who was now quite near the bush, pulled back the leaves, and looked inside.

"Lydia!" he shouted.

Lydia pressed her hands to her head.

"Franz, what is it?"

"Lydia, it's a baby!"

"What did you say?"

"It's a baby! Come and see, quick!"

She was already beside him.

"Oh, but he's not crying any more," she said. "Franz, do you think he's dead?"

"Lift him up. I'll hold the branches back so they don't get in your way."

She pushed her way through the thickly-clustered leaves and saw a carry-cot, half overturned on top of the tiny creature feebly waving its arms.

Bending down, she lifted him up and gently brought him out into the open. He was wearing diapers, a white woolen sweater, and cotton rompers embroidered with flowers. A white woolen cloak with a hood, soaked and

18

spattered with mud, was fastened around his neck. The eyes in his small delicate face were swollen and red with crying. He was quite still now, and his hands were icy cold.

Lydia sat down on a boulder and began to rock him.

"Franz, he's all wet, his clothes are soaked, and he's frozen . . . I'm afraid he may be dead."

"It seems to me," said Franz, "that we ought to take his wet things off, and rub him hard to get the blood circulating again, and then we can wrap him up in my coat. I won't need it. I've got plenty of clothes on."

Lydia undressed the baby as quickly as she could, and while Franz rubbed vigorously at the little arms and legs that were blue with cold, Lydia breathed softly on his forehead and his mouth, as she had done the previous night to bring Franz around. After a while, the child seemed to revive, then he clenched his fists and finally opened his eyes with an exhausted cry.

"He's alive!" said Lydia, hugging him. "He's opened his eyes!"

"Quick, wrap him up," Franz said.

Lydia wrapped him in the coat, turning up the ends.

"Have you got a safety pin?"

"Yes, I think there's one in my pocket."

"There," she said. "Now he'll be warm. But we ought to feed him. Isn't he lovely? Look how black his hair is! How old do you think he is?"

"He's very small. Two or three months, I should think."

"Let's make for the village as quickly as we can. Go and get his carry-cot."

When she mentioned the village, Franz again felt anxious and apprehensive. He pushed his way into the bushes and picked up the carry-cot.

"I'll carry him in my arms," said Lydia. "He won't be so

19

frightened then. Look, he's put his head against my shoulder."

"As you like," said Franz. "I'll carry the cot."

And they began their journey.

3

THEY WALKED on. Lydia held the baby close to her, and Franz, whose leg was very painful, held on to her shoulder. Their progress was slow, for they were worn out with hunger and exhaustion. The carry-cot weighed heavily on Franz's arm, and the baby on Lydia's. He cried weakly for a while and then fell asleep with his head against her shoulder.

The sun had climbed above the peaks, and now flooded the stony fields and all the surrounding mountains. As they drew near the village, they became aware of birds singing among the leafy branches of the trees.

"Franz, how did this little baby get into the bushes?"

"How did we get here ourselves?" Franz replied.

"I know. What did happen? What did happen to us?"

"There's no point in thinking about it. At least we're not alone any more, there are three of us. That's enough to go on with right now."

"That's odd," said Lydia. "There's no one about."

Franz did not answer.

"Franz, don't you think it's a strange sort of village?"

"Yes," he said gravely. "It *is* a strange sort of village. Lydia, listen — I've got something to tell you, but I don't want you to cry."

"I'll try not to," she said, but her eyes filled with tears.

"Lydia — I think the village is empty."

"I know. There's no one here, is there?"

"No, you can see for yourself . . . there's no smoke coming from the chimneys . . . Look, the street is all overgrown with grass."

"Franz, it's a deserted village, isn't it?"

"Yes, I believe it is. I know that it happens sometimes, in the mountains."

"What are we going to do?"

"We're going to have to look after ourselves," he said grimly.

"Let's make a thorough search. There may be someone left, in one house, perhaps?"

"There's not an animal to be seen, not even a hen. There isn't a sound, and not a single cultivated field. You can see, it's all run wild."

In silence they went along the grass-grown street between the houses. Roofs were sagging, and tall-growing bushes were springing up even inside the houses, thrusting their branches through the windows.

It was a narrow village, just a single street with two small lanes cutting across it. One of them climbed up to a tiny church, its door shut. Here and there were traces of gardens, now overrun with weeds. The two children, despairing, stopped walking, and looked at the landscape. The stony moorland over which they had come stretched as far as the eye could see until it met the sky. Around them in a semi-circle stood the unbroken chain of tall and solemn mountains, grim and stark even with the sun on

them. The awe-inspiring silence seemed to hum with a silken sound in their ears. Franz cupped his hands around his mouth and yelled, "Hello! Hello-o-o!"

The sound echoed through the mountains, bouncing back at them until it faded away. "Hello! Hello-o-o!" And that was all.

"Is anyone here?"

The echo repeated several times. "Anyone here? Anyone here? Here?" It was like the ripples sent out by a pebble thrown into water.

Then Franz yelled with all his might:

"Help! Help!"

But only the echo answered, and it was as though the high indifferent mountains were laughing at them. The cry for help died away in the distance, and there was only the silken sound of silence to be heard. Then Lydia, exhausted, sat down suddenly on the church steps. Tears rolled slowly down her cheeks, and fell on the face of the sleeping baby.

"Please don't cry," Franz begged.

"Franz, what's going to happen? Are we going to die?"

He forced himself to laugh, and said in a gay voice, "Of course not! People don't die so easily!"

"I'm terribly hungry. And the baby is nearly dead already."

Franz looked at the baby's face. It was very pale, with blue shadows below the closed eyelids.

"Before we do anything else," he said, "we must find some water. I do know that you can last a long time without food, but not without water."

"If only there were some sort of path, we could follow it, and it would be bound to lead somewhere."

"I'd already thought of that, but there just isn't one."

24

The baby's breathing grew shallow and seemed to miss a beat now and again. His eyes opened, and then his mouth, as though he wanted to cry; but he had no more strength, and his head lolled against Lydia's arm.

"He can't even cry any more. He's going to die," she said.

"Look, stay here and wait for me. Don't move away! See that little wood just beyond the houses? There may be a stream, it's greener there than anywhere else. I'll go and see."

"All right, but how will you bring the water back to us? I'd rather go with you."

"Yes, you're right, you'd better come with me — but are you sure you're not too tired? Shall I carry the baby?"

"No — remember your leg."

"That doesn't matter, I can take him all the same. My arms are stronger than yours."

But the baby wouldn't go to Franz. He put his head down on Lydia's shoulder and with all his small strength hung on to her coat.

"Oh, he doesn't want to leave me!" she cried, astounded. "Look how he's clinging to me!"

"You keep him then. He looks so fragile we'd better not do anything to upset him just now. We'll go slowly, and rest when we have to."

They walked along the grass-grown street between the rows of dilapidated houses, without speaking. As they reached the end of it, they heard a light musical sound breaking the immense silence.

"Lydia — can you hear that?"

"It sounds like water — like a fountain," she said.

"It's just by the wood, as I thought."

On the fringe of the trees a spring ran, sparkling and

25

crystalline, from mossy banks overgrown with wild flowers into a basin that looked as though it had been specially shaped from the rough moorland stone. From there it overflowed into a waterfall which fed a stream pursuing a course hollowed out by time. The children stood there a moment, admiring the scene. The sun glanced through the leafy trees and transformed the water to diamonds flashing in a cloud of rainbow spray. After the wasteland, the waterfall seemed friendly and gay.

"Lydia, isn't it wonderful? Here's a stream alive and singing. We're not on our own any more. Dip your hand in. Isn't it cold? We'll have to drink very slowly."

"It's so clear," said Lydia, leaning over. "I can see my reflection as if it were a mirror."

"This is a sign that there's no need to lose heart. We haven't been here very long and we've already found water. Come on, have some," he added, cupping his hands and lifting them dripping wet to Lydia's lips.

She drank several times, and while Franz was having his turn, she filled her own hands for the baby. But he turned his head away each time she tried to pour the water into his mouth.

"Have you got a handkerchief?" she asked Franz.

He looked in his pockets. "Yes, here's one."

"Soak it in the water, then I'll give it to him to suck, like a bottle. I think he'll understand then."

As soon as the baby discovered the corner of the soaked handkerchief on his tongue, he found enough energy to suck it, clinging to Lydia's hand with both of his so that she would not take it away.

"How thirsty he is!" she said.

They soaked the handkerchief in the stream several times, and as soon as the baby grew accustomed again to drinking, Lydia squeezed the water straight into his mouth

26

so that he could take more of it. Then she made him comfortable in the coat she had wrapped him in, and rocked him gently until he fell asleep.

Afterwards Franz and Lydia looked at each other very seriously. They realized that they were now on their own, with no one to look after them in this vast wilderness surrounded by the harsh mountains. Henceforward they could rely only on each other, and the hours and the days would be exactly what they had the courage to make them. They must either struggle and survive, or lie down and die.

"In any case," Lydia suddenly spoke, unconsciously voicing aloud the conclusion she had reached, "it's not only us; there's the baby. He's so much smaller and weaker than we are, even more lost than we are — he can't do anything for himself. He will depend on us for everything."

"That's exactly what I was thinking. We've got to struggle through this for him too, not only for ourselves."

"I promise I won't cry any more," Lydia vowed, lifting her pale face to Franz.

"And I'll promise to help you as much as I can, and I'll never leave you on your own," said Franz.

"Let's shake hands on it then," she said, "— the baby too, poor thing! If we all three promise to stay together and help each other, we'll feel better right away."

Franz and Lydia solemnly shook hands, and then touched the baby's hand; and all at once, in spite of their exhaustion and hunger, and the agonizing uncertainty that hung over them, they felt happy and at peace, as though some change had taken place. They looked at each other again, and now their eyes were sparkling, as though the sun and the water and their new pact had brought them back to life.

Lydia put the sleeping baby carefully down on the soft

moss; then she came across to Franz, saying with a certain firmness in her voice, "The first thing to do now is to have a look at your leg."

He rolled up his long trousers. His leg was stained from knee to ankle with dried blood from a cut that looked as though it had gone deep. His sock was stiff with blood, and his shoe spattered with it.

"I'll wash it first," Lydia said. "I must have a hanky somewhere."

She found one in the pocket of her coat.

When the wound had been cleaned they discovered that it was not as big as they had thought. The blood that covered his leg had made it look much worse than it was.

"Let the sun get to it for a while, then I'll try to put a bandage on it."

Franz did as he was told, stretching his leg out in front of him, and once more they fell silent. It grew warmer as time passed. Beyond the wood that sheltered them they could see the rocky moorland shimmering with heat haze. The air was delicately scented by the mosses and the slender plants that clustered at the foot of the trees, their lilac flowers half hidden in the leaves.

"How odd," Lydia said. "There aren't any midges."

"We must be very high up," Franz said. "There aren't any insects above — well, two thousand feet."

Mingling with the scent of the damp mosses was the sharp tangy smell from a cluster of pines, their trunks studded with gleaming drops of resin, and glowing red in the sunlight.

"Smell!" said Lydia, her eyes closed. "Smell how beautiful it is!"

"Yes, it's wonderful," said Franz, and he too closed his eyes and flung back his head.

"Do you know, I'm not the slightest bit miserable any more," Lydia said suddenly. "I wonder why? And I'm not at all afraid, either. If I weren't so hungry, I'd be enjoying myself. Why, Franz?"

"I don't know," he said. And to himself he thought, "I'm enjoying myself too. Why? Everything's as ghastly as it could possibly be, there's no hope of any help within reach. And we're utterly alone, and lost. We may be going to die in this very spot and no one will ever know, a ghastly death, one after the other — and yet I feel terrifically happy!"

"What are you thinking about, Franz?"

"Nothing, it's pleasant here."

"I'd better bandage your leg now."

The handkerchief she had spread over a stone was almost dry. She folded it lengthwise and put it carefully over the gash. Then she wound the belt from her dress around the injured leg and tied it firmly.

"Thank you," said Franz. "You're a marvelous nurse! It feels much better — I'll be able to walk now."

"I'm too hot," Lydia said. "I'm going to wrap the baby in my coat. It's thinner than yours and it will fold more easily."

While she was changing them over she felt something bulky and hard she hadn't noticed before, in the pocket of Franz's coat. She put in her hand and, unbelievably, took out a package of biscuits.

"Franz, look!"

"Biscuits!"

She gave him one and bit into another herself.

"Biscuits . . . didn't you know they were in your pocket?"

"Since I can't remember anything, I suppose I'd forgotten that too."

"I'm going to have three and so are you, three. We'll give two to the baby, and save the rest."

"Do you think he'll be able to eat them?"

"I'll crush them up in the palm of my hand and mix them with a little water. I'll try to make him eat it like baby food."

"While you're doing that," Franz said, "I'll go back to the place where we slept. We left so quickly this morning that we didn't even look around. We were only thinking of getting to the village. But since there's no one here and we're really on our own now, I must go back and search it thoroughly. I might find something that would explain . . . I might even find someone who got there the same way we did, someone who would help us . . ."

"Don't leave me! I want to go with you."

"No, there's no sense in that for any of us. You'll be much better here, where it's cool. Don't move from here. Just be brave and wait for me."

"All right," she said, trying not to cry and realizing that she must do what he said.

"I'll come back as soon as I possibly can, I promise."

"We'll be waiting," she said, without any fuss.

"Have another biscuit. You must be starving. So long, then! And don't worry."

"Don't leave us alone all night!"

"I'll be back long before then, so don't get worked up!"

He seized a branch, and stripped it to make a walking stick that would help him over the rocky moorland with his injured leg.

Standing at the edge of the wood, Lydia, heavy-hearted, watched him walk into the distance, along the deserted grass-grown street between the crumbling houses.

31

4

LYDIA, ALONE, was seized with panic, and she wondered what had become of the happiness she had felt such a little while before. When Franz was there, everything was all right; but as soon as he disappeared beyond the last house, a strange sadness fell upon the place. The sunlight was dimmed, the sound of the stream was melancholy, the scented air became oppressive, and an atmosphere of disquiet hung over the wood that only a moment before had been so sunny and so fresh. The mountains were menacing, the sky brazen, and minutes grew long and heavy, while despair weighed her down, spread and overwhelmed her completely until she could no longer endure it.

"Franz!" she called. "Franz!"

She started to run after him, but the thought of the baby brought her to a halt. She returned to the stream, shaking all over. The baby was still sleeping, rolled up in his improvised blanket, and from time to time he cried a little. It was quite impossible to leave him there, and even more impossible to try to catch up with Franz carrying the baby in her arms.

Lydia sat on a stone beside him. Her heart was beating so fast she felt she would suffocate, her hands were frozen, and a cold sweat had broken out on her forehead. Her face grew strained as she wondered how she could overcome this panic of mind and body. It was the thought of Franz that brought her to her senses. She must stop being so silly or he would know what a coward she was. He himself had gone off alone to try to find some solution to their dreadful predicament. And he had done this in spite of his hurt leg, his hunger and weariness, and the heat of the midday sun. She could not let him come back, worn out, to find only her tear-stained face, and realize that she was one more burden. She could not add to his own anxiety by showing hers, and making him feel even more lost and more unhappy than he would have felt by himself.

She had promised never to cry again. She would fight against her terror; she would overcome the terrible despair that filled her mind. But she was so afraid that he wouldn't come back, and wondered what would become of her then, alone with the baby. Wild animals might attack them. There might well be bears in these mountains, or starving wolves, or eagles.

She got up and looked around apprehensively. She must certainly be dying, for no one could live with a heart that beat as fast as hers.

Then all at once she thrust her hands into the pockets of her dress, squared her shoulders and stared steadily at the sharp-toothed mountains.

"That's enough," she said out loud. "Franz must come back. He will come back, I know he will. And until it's dark I won't even think that he might not come. And if he does, I don't want him to find me dead just because I wasn't brave enough to wait for him. If I'm silly enough to die of fright before he gets back, who's going to welcome him and see that he rests? Who will look after his bad leg?"

She would prove that she was not a coward. This very day she would show what she was capable of doing. Somehow she must arrange things so that Franz would feel happier when he returned. She must find shelter for the night. And then she would wash in the stream and tidy her tousled hair, and bathe the baby, who certainly needed attention.

When he came back, Franz should find them both neat and clean and willing to set out, if he had found a path. And by keeping busy she might also forget to be frightened.

The baby began to cry. Lydia crumbled two biscuits in her hand and moistened them with water. She took him in her arms and carefully put some of the improvised baby food on his tongue. He seemed to like it, and little by little he swallowed it all. In this way she made him eat two biscuits, then a third, and then she gave him the handkerchief soaked in water to suck, so that he could drink too. Taking advantage of the sun that warmed the boulders around the little pool, she unfastened the coat, took off the dirty diaper he was still wearing, washed it in the stream and spread it on a warm rock to dry. The baby seemed to find this funny, for he kicked his small legs in the air and waved his arms about, gurgling with joy. He turned his head and stared at Lydia with his slanting eyes. He looked so enchanting, that for a moment Lydia forgot her loneliness.

As soon as she had bathed him, she rubbed him quickly all over with her woolen scarf, so that he wouldn't catch cold. He began to chuckle and then to laugh. Birds came to perch on the branches above them and sang with lively voices that sounded like the notes of a flute.

"What a pretty baby you are!" Lydia said. "You've got such lovely, smooth black hair — oh, yes, you're very pretty.

Franz will come back to us, you'll see. He'll have found something. Everything's going to be all right, and you'll find your mother again. So don't worry, I'll look after you until your mother comes!"

When he was really warm, she wrapped him once more in her coat and put him down on a soft mossy bed, in the shade. He became absorbed in the fluttering of the leaves above his head and seemed to be talking to them.

"I'll wash his clothes in the stream too," Lydia thought, "and put them out to dry while there's still some sun."

She suddenly felt so ravenous that before she began she ate two more biscuits. She counted the ones that were left: fourteen. Franz would need some this evening. He would be so tired, he could easily eat five; then two for her and two for the baby. That left only five for tomorrow morning before they set off on the road that Franz would have discovered.

It was good to keep busy like this; it stopped her feeling lonely. Look after the baby, think about Franz, make the best of everything and so chase away the spectre of fear and keep up one's courage. When she had eaten her biscuits, she closed the package carefully and put it beside the baby. Then she began to wash his things.

She spread them along a low wall just beyond the wood. The sun blazed down and the wall was hot. "They'll dry quickly," she thought. Then she went back into the wood and undressed and bathed. It was fun to dip her feet into the green water that was so clear she could see her reflection in it. The baby chattered away in his own language, and so did the birds.

She dried herself as well as she could with leaves she tore from a low-hanging branch and then went out into the sun. It was so hot that she was completely dry almost at once. The cold water and the sun did her good. She felt stronger, much readier to be brave and not disgrace Franz. Her hair was drawn up to the top of her head and held there by a wide comb. She let it down and combed it, using the pool as a mirror.

The wood grew thicker on the other side of the stream, climbing up the mountainside. Some tall pines shut out the sight of what lay beyond. Lydia decided she would explore the wood a little while waiting for Franz. It would be a pleasant walk, and help to fill in the time. She took the baby in her arms and walked toward the pines. The place attracted her. On the slope the interlaced roots of the trees were like steps, and it was easy to climb them.

She expected to find still more wooded land behind the pines, and she was looking forward to watching squirrels frisk about, or picking the petals off the daisies, or maybe gathering wild strawberries. But when she had climbed the last step she found herself on a sort of terrace that must at one time have been a garden. There were traces of flowerbeds, now overgrown with brushwood; garden flowers had grown tall on their slender stems in their search for the sun, and there were still signs of pathways beneath the coarse silvery grasses. A small house, apparently shut up, but not falling to pieces like those in the village, stood at the far end. The chimney just showed above the low roof with its wide eaves. Roses that had gone back to their natural state grew about the door in riotous abandon. A thick square shutter covered a window to the right of the door.

Just a little afraid, Lydia approached the house and walked around it. The wood ended there, and behind the house a steep field climbed up the mountainside in a scatter of rolling pebbles.

The baby was asleep again, his head lolling against

Lydia's shoulder. She went back to the terrace and looked around on all sides. Silence, silence, unbelievable silence. The mountains seemed to dance in the shimmering light and the tallest of them were capped with snow. Solitude weighed her down. With all her heart Lydia longed to see some sort of animal. Even a lizard would be welcome if she could only see one darting among the stones, though she didn't like them at all. But there was no one except herself and her shadow stretching along the silvery grass of the ghostly paths. She went up to the house, peering in through a crack in the door, and as she leaned against it, she was astonished to feel the door yield and slowly half open. Yet she had to push against it with all her strength to open it farther, for the wood had swollen.

Inside she found a square, gloomy room. Somehow the light of day coming in seemed unusual there. A damp cold and the smell of mildew came from it. Lydia was afraid the baby would be too cold, so she left him on the step in front of the door, folding the sleeve of the coat in which he was wrapped to make a pillow for his head. Then she kissed him on his round cheek, near the blue shadows under his closed eyes. The feel of his smooth warm face gave her new courage and took away some of the despair in her heart. She went into the house, into more solitude and silence. A black fireplace filled the whole of one wall; it still showed traces of long dead fires. In the opposite wall was a cupboard with two rough wooden doors. There was a kind of bed in one corner, and a crude table made from a dark unpolished plank of wood set on two knotty tree trunks, surrounded by four stools. That was all.

Lydia opened the window and pushed back the shutter. She had to use both hands, for it was very heavy and the rusty hinges would not give. It yielded at last with a loud groan as it fell back against the wall. The dazzling sun filled the room with its dancing dust motes and came to rest on the old red flagstones of the floor.

"If Franz comes back too late for us to set out at once," Lydia thought, unconsciously clasping her hands together, "we can sleep here. We'll be dry here if it rains, and safe from wild animals."

She crossed the room slowly, walking on tiptoe as though she were afraid of disturbing someone. Even though no one was there, she felt as though she were prying. The cupboard in the wall was not fastened — it had no key — and in it there were some kitchen things — a cooking pot, an earthenware dish, a big pitcher and a smaller one, a number of basins, some bowls, and two earthenware mugs. There was also a pile of thick coarse folded blankets. It was as though whoever had lived in that house had left everything ready for his return, and then had never come back.

"I'll get everything ready for tonight," Lydia said to herself. "It won't be so bad if we can sleep here. How pleased Franz will be!"

She began to smile and clap her hands as she thought what a surprise it would be for him.

The blankets were damp. With considerable difficulty, for they were very heavy, Lydia carried them into the garden and spread them out in the sun. Then she went back into the house and took all the pots and pans out of the cupboard. At the back of it, all along the wall, fungi were growing. Lydia swept the shelves thoroughly with a crudely-made broom she found in the bottom of the cupboard, and then left the doors wide open to air it and dry out the cellar-like dampness. Then she picked up the cooking pot to go down to the stream to fetch some water

to wash the dishes in. The baby slept on the doorstep, the little garden was tranquil, and a gentle breeze set the grasses swaying. There were no insects, no wild life other than the birds, so Lydia thought she would leave the baby for a moment and take the dishes down to the stream and wash them there. She put the bowls and basins into the cooking pot, then picked it up and began the descent. At the bottom of the steps the stream was still babbling and falling into the green waters of the pool in a shower of silver spray that sprinkled the mosses and the mauve flowers. The baby's clothes, spread on the wall, were bone dry. Lydia carefully folded them, then washed the dishes in the pool. When this was done she filled the largest pitcher with clean fresh water, and carried everything up to the terrace again, stopping to rest from time to time, for the pitcher was heavy and so was the cooking pot. When she got back she felt that the house already had a welcoming air. The baby was still sleeping on the threshold, which was now in shadow. The door and shutter flung wide and the blankets spread out on the ground seemed to show that the house was coming to life.

"We could call it *Our Home*" Lydia thought. She imagined the name painted in green, beside the door, and she began to laugh.

She would have to hurry to put everything in order, and to have it all ready in time. The sun had already retreated to the other end of the garden, and Franz couldn't be back early enough for them to start out that evening. Lydia picked up the blankets, now dry and warm to her touch, and carried them into the house. There was a mattress on the bed, filled with something like seeds, that slid about as she moved it. It was patched but it was clean, and when she had made up the bed, it looked quite different. She put the pots and pans back into the cupboard, and then she ran out into the garden and picked some flowers, arranged them in a jug and put them on the table.

"That looks pretty. It's just like a party." Then she thought — "That box by the fireplace. I didn't see it before. It will make a lovely cradle for the baby."

She dragged it outside, cleaned it out with the broom, half filled it with hay she had discovered in a lean-to shed at the back of the house, and pushed it beside the bed. Then she looked around at her handiwork. The room looked really lived-in; it was quite charming. And now she must go and see if Franz were coming along the road, for she didn't want him to be alarmed at not finding her by the stream.

Just then the baby woke and began to cry. Lydia lifted him up, and gave him some water and a little biscuit. That seemed to satisfy him, and she carried him down the steps to the path where Franz had set out. The sun was low in the sky, and now that the grass-grown street was in shadow it looked still more desolate and even colder than it had before. Lydia walked on, her weight thrown back because of the baby. She sensed something in the air that warned her of the coming of night. Now that the sun was gone, the deserted houses looked sinister, and the branches thrusting through the roofs and the windows seemed ready to grab her. And all at once the terrible despair, that the afternoon's work had kept at bay, descended upon her once more.

She was terrified by the loneliness of this phantom street in the high mountains. The pinewood darkened as the day drew to an end. The birds had fled. The silence was so absolute that Lydia could hear the blood pulsing in her ears, and sounds that came only from her imagination.

41

When she had passed the last derelict house, she sat down on a crumbling wall. From that point she could see the path crossing the stony moorland until it came to a turning beyond which it disappeared. They had come that way in the morning and Franz must return along it, since he knew no other route.

Shivering on the low wall, hugging the baby to her, Lydia imagined that the mountains were dancing a devil's dance about her as nightfall approached. Hunger and terror made her feel dizzy, and she was afraid she would not be able to hold the sleeping baby much longer.

"If only Franz would come back," she thought. "What if he's lost? What if he can't find the way? Oh, I should never have let him go. We should all have gone together! If he doesn't come back, what will become of us, the baby and me? Suppose his leg starts bleeding again and hurts so much that he can't walk? Oh, I should never have let him go!"

"Franz!" she called. "Franz!"

Her voice was so thin and weak that the echo flung it back from mountain to mountain like the bleating of an animal. "Fra-an-anz! We're here. Can you hear me?"

And the echo repeated, "Hear me — me — me." Then there was silence again.

Nearly frantic, Lydia screamed, "Hello! Hello! Hello!"

Then, just as she was about to give up, worn out and half-fainting, she heard, quite plainly, a real voice calling in the distance, through the echo.

"Hello! Hello!"

Lydia leaned against the wall for support.

"Franz!" she yelled with all her might.

A long way off and below her a faint voice cried, "Lydia!"

"Franz!"

"Lydia!"

"Hello! Hello!"

"Hello!"

Lydia burst into tears all over the baby. "It's Franz!" she told him, as if he could understand. "Do you hear? Franz is there . . . he isn't lost, he'll be here soon."

Even as she wept, her panic faded. The pines didn't seem so dark, the mountains stopped whirling round and the sinister countryside became almost friendly.

She walked farther along the path, for she no longer felt tired. Beyond the turning, she could see Franz, so far away he looked very small. He stopped, and waved his hand wildly. Lydia waved hers in reply. Franz set off again. He appeared to be dragging something very heavy behind him. He must be tired, for he stopped often; but each time he waved his hand, and Lydia found this completely reassuring.

She forgot all her woes — fear, hunger, uncertainty, even the night that would soon be on them. Franz came steadily on, dragging his mysterious load. She watched him as he came, her mind at ease, feeling safe once more.

As he came nearer she saw that he was pulling a sort of wooden packing-case behind him. He was hauling it over the rough stones by his leather belt passed through two slats.

"Hurrah!" he shouted as he drew near.

"Franz!"

Just the sight of him returning gave her renewed energy and a feeling of security. He was only a child, not much stronger than she was, lost with her in the middle of a vast unyielding wilderness, but while he was there, she could endure anything. Putting the baby on the ground, she flung herself on Franz as though he were her father coming

43

home from work. His face was streaming with sweat, and he stayed still a moment to get his breath back.

"I'm so glad you came to meet me. I was just wondering whether I'd be able to get as far as the stream on my own. Finding you here makes all the difference."

Then he began to chuckle.

"See what I've found!"

"What is it?"

"A packing-case. It's terribly heavy, it's got all sorts of things inside."

"And what's in that sack on your shoulder?"

"Oh, it's wonderful! If you only knew! When I left you I went through the village and I walked and walked and walked. I passed the place where we found each other yesterday evening, but there was no sign of anyone. It was just as deserted as it was this morning. *No clue of any kind.* So I went on, following a little path, quite by chance. It led upwards . . . it was very difficult, believe me! I don't know how far I climbed."

She listened, her head a little on one side, eager to know what happened next.

"All at once the path disappeared. But I had to go on, because I'd caught sight of a sort of hut. I just had to look inside it, didn't I?"

"Of course. And then?"

"Then I went on a few yards over the stones and the rocks until I reached the hut."

"Was there anyone there?"

"No, no one, but there were lots of things inside. We could have slept there, but it would be quite impossible for you to climb up to it, to say nothing of the baby."

"But Franz, what sort of things were inside?"

"Well, there was some furniture of course, but best of

44

all there was a cupboard! I looked inside — and that's when the miracle happened." He was laughing. The lock of fair hair fell down over his eyes and his face so lit up that he didn't seem exhausted any longer. Lydia laughed with him, not knowing what it was all about, just because he was laughing.

"Oh, do tell me quickly!"

"Well — in that cupboard there was everything you could want to make a meal: a camp stove, meat cubes, all sorts of food, cans, and a can-opener, packages of biscuits. You'll see, it's terrific. Oh, Lydia, it was such a relief!"

"You're sure there was no one there? If the owner comes back, Franz, he'll think you've burgled his hut."

"No, no, it doesn't belong to anyone. I'm quite sure what it is — it's an Alpine hut, a shelter for climbers when they're taken by surprise in a storm and have to spend the night there, or a few days . . . And when you come to think of it, that's just what's happened to us, isn't it?"

Lydia looked around at the high peaks fading into the darkness.

"That's true. We're just like those climbers. It's not really stealing, is it, Franz?"

"Of course not, that's what I said to myself. While I was looking around I saw this empty packing-case. There are some more there too. I put as much as I could into it, everything I thought would be most useful, that we needed most urgently. I'll show you — oh, it's marvelous!"

"Franz, you must be exhausted."

"Yes, I'm all in. And I'm starving. But I did so want to tell you what was in the box."

"I was so frightened without you . . . but you're here now, and I'm not a bit scared any more."

"I think we should go back to the stream; we're better

45

off there — with the water and the cans in this sack we can have some milk. Luckily the weather's all right, so if we huddle up close to each other, all three of us, we can keep warm enough to get to sleep. If only you could climb up to the hut."

Lydia turned her head away to hide the smile that she could not keep back, but all she said was, "Yes, of course, let's go back to the stream."

5

THE WAY back seemed shorter, though as daylight faded the grass-grown street was filled with ghosts, until Franz suddenly said, "Let's sing!"

"Yes, let's," Lydia replied. "It will help us along."

"I'll begin," said Franz, and in a voice hoarse with weariness he struck up with, *"Ten green bottles hanging on a wall — ten green bottles hanging on a wall —"*

"And if one green bottle should accidentally fall —" Lydia took up the song, and then together they sang — *"There'd be nine green bottles hanging on the wall."*

"Nine green bottles hanging on the wall
Nine green bottles hanging on the wall
And if one green bottle should accidentally fall
There'd be eight green bottles hanging on the wall."

Their feet picked up the rhythm of the song, they forgot how tired they were, and without noticing, they quickened their pace. The mountains on their right were rose-pink and the dark pines glowed red.

"Eight green bottles hanging on the wall
Eight green bottles hanging on the wall —"

On their left the mountain peaks were gray and made

47

them think of wild dogs crouching. Behind Franz, the packing-case scraped over the paving stones.

"And if one green bottle should accidentally fall
There'd be seven green bottles hanging on the wall."

Into the vast silence, where even the birds made no sound, their small voices rose, forlorn and yet somehow heroic, the only sign of life where no other life existed.

"Seven green bottles hanging on the wall
Seven green bottles hanging on the wall —"

"The worst thing, Lydia, was hauling the box over the rocks and boulders."

"I honestly don't know how you managed it, Franz, all by yourself with your leg!"

"Oh, my leg is much better!" he answered bravely. "I pushed and I pulled and I heaved, and got stuck on the biggest rocks — I don't know how I did it! But it's unbelievable, what you can do when you have to!"

Like a lamp going out, the last rosy glow disappeared, and darkness fell, frightening, heavy, and full of menace. They began singing again, and their voices shook a little —

"Six green bottles hanging on the wall
Six green bottles hanging on the wall —"

A long way away, miles beyond these woods and mountain peaks, this moorland and this sky, miles beyond other woods, other mountains, other moors, there were towns lit up with twinkling lights at this hour of the day. There were roads too, and other children, coming out of school, walked along them to their homes and families. All over the world they would be singing songs like this one, in all sorts of languages, in towns, where thousands of people were ready to help children in trouble, as parents always do.

But here there was only solitude, the nightmare of a cruel and terrifying solitude.

"Five green bottles hanging on the wall
Five green bottles hanging on the wall —"
And the two small voices in harmony —
"And if one green bottle should accidentally fall —"
When they reached the stream, Lydia did not stop, but went on climbing.

"Where are you going?"

She turned and smiled over her shoulder.

"It'll soon be pitch dark, Lydia."

"That's why we must hurry," she said. "Come on!"

"But why go any farther?"

"You'll see."

"Have you found something?"

"Maybe."

She laughed and went on. He followed her, leaving the packing-case. The bottom of the garden was drowned in shadow, but the little house could still be seen against the fading light. Franz looked at it, his eyes widening as he wondered if he were dreaming.

"Is anyone there?" he said.

"No, no one. It's our house, Franz, for tonight."

Now that the sun had gone, an indefinable cold seeped down from the glaciers in the folds of the mountains. The children shivered, tired and hungry.

"Let's get in quickly," Lydia urged. "We'll be safe inside."

She pushed the door open and put the sleeping baby on the bed. Franz went back to get the packing-case, and Lydia helped him.

"You found a house," Franz said, as they came back. "Oh, Lydia, what luck!"

And he added, sighing, "I'm so tired!"

"Yes, isn't it wonderful luck? I cleaned everything, and

49

got it all ready. It's very nice, you know! I do wish you could see it. We need some light."

"There are matches and candles in the sack." He went to the little window, through which filtered a gray light, and burrowed in the sack. He lit two candles, and as the flame sprang up, friendly and reassuring, they looked at each other, laughing, and dazzled by the sudden brilliance.

"Put them on the chimney piece."

Lydia took two glasses from the cupboard, climbed on to a stool, and placed one candle on the chimney piece, then another on the table.

"It looks fine," said Franz. "Did you put the flowers there?"

"Yes, and I've made up the bed too. I found some blankets. We'll sleep better than on the ground by the stream."

"Quick, let's get some food out of the sack."

"I'll set the table."

Lydia took two bowls and the two mugs from the cupboard and put them on the table.

"Here's the camp stove," shouted Franz, "and there's a saucepan too."

The water came quickly to a boil. The familiar sound filled the room as the steam rose up.

Lydia put some powdered milk into a basin and mixed it with water into a fine creamy white liquid.

"Look, I found this little empty bottle. I thought it might do for a feeding bottle."

"Oh good. Is there still some water in the saucepan?"

"Yes."

"But there's no nipple! Oh well, never mind, I'll use the handkerchief."

Once the baby was awake, he smelled the milk and seized the improvised feeder with two greedy hands, sucking at the corner of the soaked handkerchief.

50

"Better not give him all of it," Franz advised. "It's a long time since he had anything, and it may upset his stomach."

Leaning over the baby, Lydia frowned with concentration as she held the bottle. She looked as though she were grappling with a very serious problem. With a toss of her head she flung back her blonde hair and looked anxiously at Franz.

"How much do you think I should give him? This much?"

The bottle was still three-quarters full.

"Yes," said Franz hesitantly, "— about that . . . I think so . . . we can give him more later."

The baby fell asleep at once. Lydia laid him carefully in his carry-cot, which she had put in the box half filled with hay, and covered him with his hooded cloak. Franz watched her gravely.

"He looks better already," he whispered. "And so contented."

"He's got nothing to worry about," Lydia whispered back, "he relies on us."

"I wish I were like him!" Franz's sudden show of weakness, the first since they had met, startled Lydia. She looked at him and saw how pale he was, his eyes dark-ringed. Sheer exhaustion dragged down the corners of his mouth and gave his face the bitterness of a man's. He was leaning forward, with one hand over his leg as though it hurt him. His fair hair, damp with sweat, fell across his eyes.

"I rely on him, too," she thought. "He's carrying all our burdens, and it's more than he can bear. He walked all that way without food; his leg hurts; and how tired he looks!"

"You sit down at once," she said. "I'll take care of everything. We're going to have something to eat, then we'll go to sleep, and we'll be as happy as the baby. He relies on

52

us. And I rely on you. So you must rely on me, don't you think?"

She said this half smiling, and looked affectionately at him, then took him by the hand and led him to the table. They sat down facing each other.

"I'm longing to see everything in the box, but that can wait until tomorrow. Tonight you must rest."

6

THERE WAS such a wonderful feeling of being safe. In a few moments terror and weariness melted away. The door was well and truly fastened against whatever might threaten outside. Inside, the candles were lit, cozy and reassuring. There were three of them, counting the fragile little creature sleeping trustfully in his improvised cot: there were above all the two of them, ready to cheer each other up and face things together as best they could. Eagerly and in silence they drank their bowls of hot milk. Franz brought rusks and biscuits, canned butter and chocolate out of the box.

"We mustn't eat it all," he said. "We must think of tomorrow — we may have to stay here a day or two."

As soon as they had finished eating they began to fall asleep. Lydia's eyelids fluttered and then closed for a moment. Franz felt his head swinging like a pendulum.

"Let's go to bed quickly," he said. "What luck that you found this house! Come and look outside, it's pitch black."

Lydia went to the window. He had opened the wooden shutter, and she stood on tiptoe, leaning against his shoulder. It was dark, with no moon. They could only guess at the tall shapes of the mountains, their outlines gleaming faintly with snow. The air was damp, and much colder than the night before; there was absolute silence.

"Oh, Franz — suppose we were still out in the open! — even near the stream!"

"Let's close it quickly."

Lydia looked at the baby, covered him carefully and kissed him good night. He was warm and breathing quietly, and his pink cheeks made him look healthy. She put the rest of his feed in a corner of his cot, under the little mattress, to keep it warm. Franz put out one candle and brought the other near the bed. They lay down fully dressed on the hard bunk, which seemed to them most comfortable. Franz put out the light and they drew the thick woolen blankets, that still smelled faintly of mildew, up to their chins.

"Good night, Franz."

"Good night, Lydia."

She held his hand. They fell asleep at once.

Franz woke first. Lydia was still sleeping, her fair hair spread about her face.

"I wonder what time it is," Franz said to himself. He got up quietly, opened the door, and was dazzled by the light outside. In front of him, a green slope flooded with sunlight climbed up the mountainside to a cluster of dark firs. The little garden overrun with weeds lay in the shadow and glistened with dew. Birds flew among the branches and even came as far as the doorstep, as though to greet him. There was a sharpness in the air, the smell of damp grass. Franz breathed deeply and filled his lungs with fresh air. The beauty of this new morning and the song of the birds brought him courage and made him feel happy. All would be well. Today they would discover a road leading to a real village. People would give them shelter; then, after a few days' rest, they would both remember what had happened and why they were there . . . everything would turn out all right.

Franz went back into the room, closed the door, and opened the shutter over the window.

"Lydia! Lydia! Wake up!" he called.

She sat up, startled, rubbed her eyes, then saw Franz and smiled.

"What's the time?"

"Quite late, I think, the sun's well up. It's a lovely day! You'll see, everything's going to be all right. We've got food and a house, the baby is better and I feel better too. What about you?"

"Oh, I'm fine. We're all fit enough to set out again. When are we going to look for a road?"

"As soon as possible. Let's get a move on!"

"Oh yes," she said, jumping out of bed. "Let's hurry!"

"Shall I go and wash in the stream?"

"Yes, do, while I get breakfast and make the baby's bottle."

The baby, now awake, was murmuring to himself, his voice still weak but enchanting to hear. He was waving his arms, and one leg too, that had escaped from the covers, his head turned towards Lydia, his mouth in a smile. Lydia leaned over him and watched with delight. He was soaked, so she changed him, and put him on the bed, which she had already re-made, with the blankets all smooth and neat. Then she lifted the bedding of the carry-cot, to air the sheets and turn the mattress. In doing so, she found a plastic holder, like a large and bulky envelope, that had been under the mattress. She opened it and laughed to herself when she saw what was inside. It was the baby's miniature luggage. Neatly-folded diapers, jackets, little pants, two pairs of linen rompers, two sweaters, a spare cloak longer and thicker than the one he was wearing, socks, and bootees. In the middle of it was his baby basket and two feeding bottles with a box of nipples. It was wonderful to have all these things. She lit the camp stove and put water on to boil for the milk. Then she carefully put all the treasures she had found back into their holder.

Franz came back, his face glowing, his hair damp and well slicked down.

"The water's marvelous, you've no idea. Cold, but it wakes you up all right!"

"I'm coming," said Lydia. "I'll take the pots with me and wash them. Look after the baby and the stove."

She put the used bowls into the cooking pot, and ran down to the pool, that looked even greener than it had the evening before, framed with ferns, the mauve calyxes of the flowers not yet opened to the day. Lydia plunged her hand in the icy water. Above her a bird trilled his song.

She undressed, washed swiftly all over, dried herself with a bunch of leaves, put her clothes on again, and did her hair, using the pool as a mirror. Then she cleaned her few pots with a handful of grit from the stream. She climbed up to the house, feeling refreshed.

"When she's away everything grows dark," Franz thought. "But when she comes back, it's as if she brought the sun with her."

"I've made breakfast," he said aloud.

"Oh good, I'm hungry."

"So am I."

But Lydia gave the baby his bottle before she had her own breakfast.

57

"He must be fed first," she said. "He's so tiny."

Afterwards, sitting opposite Franz and dipping her buttered rusk in her milk, she said, "Now, how are we going to set about it?"

"Finding a road?"

"Yes."

"We'll go out and look for it. It's a fine day, and we're rested now. I'll drag the box the way I did yesterday, and you can carry the baby."

"Now, Franz?"

"Yes, at once!"

They put everything they might need in the packing-case with some food. Then they wrapped the baby in his carrying cloak, and shut the door carefully behind them.

"It was nice there, last night, wasn't it, Franz? I love this house. It's been kind to us."

"I do too," Franz said. "It's put new heart into us."

Just before they left the garden, Lydia turned and blew a kiss to the kind little house with the overhanging eaves; then, following Franz, she went down the steps all slippery with pine-needles.

7

It was about the same time that the stream had welcomed them the day before. The sun was piercing through the shining leaves as it had then, and the mauve calyxes were reflected in the water. It was already a friendly and familiar scene, and, although they said nothing to each other, they were sad at having to say goodbye to it. They went along the deserted, grass-grown street, and then just before the last house, Franz turned off onto a path that went perpendicularly down between two barns with their roofs caved in.

"You think we'll be able to get down this way?"

"We'll have to see. The valley must be here somewhere, since the stream runs down in this direction. There should be villages there, even a town perhaps."

The path sloped down and came out very soon onto a meadow even more steeply sloped. The grass was uneven and their feet sank into it. The meadow led to a clump of firs perched precariously over space. It was quite impossible for them to go on that way. Franz tried to go farther, hanging on to a fir. He found himself looking down into an abyss.

"It's no good here," he said, "there's a sheer drop."

"Does that mean we'll have to climb back up the meadow?"

"I'm afraid so. Are you tired?"

"Not very," she said, "only it's difficult with the baby."

"Carry him on your back, in your coat. I'll fix it for you."

Buttoned up, and with sleeves tied together, the coat made a sort of pocket. Franz put the baby into it.

"You're right," Lydia said. "It's much better like this. He doesn't seem so heavy. And I can use my hands."

The climb to the top again was hard, and sometimes they had to go on hands and knees. They hadn't realized, when they came down, half-sitting, just how steep the meadow was. The sun beat down and they sweated under it, while there was so much heat haze that the whole countryside seemed to be going round in circles until they felt dizzy. They didn't like to tell each other how hard it was. Franz found himself dragged back by the weight of the packing-case, Lydia by the weight of the baby. They had to rest for some time when they got back to the path leading to the village, and neither of them could speak.

"How hot it is!" Franz said at last.

"Yes, it is. Do you think it's afternoon?"

"I'm afraid so. It took a long time to get down that field, and even longer to get up again."

"We must be moving again, or we'll still be on our way when night comes."

"Are you feeling better?"

"Yes, a bit. Let's go on."

"There's no point in going the way I went yesterday," Franz said. "I looked around while I was there. The plateau overhangs a valley so deep you can't see the bottom of it. There's no road at all. It's like a balcony without a railing, or a huge diving-board."

"So?"

"So there's only the right side of the village, beyond the stream. We're sure to find a road there."

Once more they walked along the grass-grown street with its gutted houses, until they came to the stream and its pleasant shade. Once more they found a rocky slope with scattered firs; and then, looking around, they saw that here too the slope overhung the abyss. The stream fell over in a graceful waterfall, rebounded from a jutting boulder, and then coursed wildly down until the eye could no longer follow it.

"There's no road here either," said Franz, and he spoke so quietly that Lydia could scarcely hear what he said. She made no attempt to reply, just stood there quite still as though she were stunned, her arms hanging down, her back bowed beneath the weight of the sleeping baby. For a long while they stood like that, facing the great mountains, themselves so small and lost and defenseless. The sun's rays were already slanting, and the light on the rocks and fir trees was uneven. It must have been long after lunchtime, but Franz and Lydia were so overwhelmed by this last catastrophe that they were neither hungry nor thirsty. The baby woke and began to cry, so Franz lifted him up and went to sit on a boulder with him while Lydia took the bottle from the box, where it had been well wrapped so that it was still warm. The baby drank energetically, and then fell asleep again. Franz and Lydia ate some rusks and chocolate. Their throats were so choked they could hardly swallow. Franz was looking at the nearest mountain: it was the one backing the plateau on which the village was built, and a rough mule track, almost overgrown, climbed along it and wound around the peak. That was clearly the only way out of this deserted region, a path that had not been used for a long time, but which must lead somewhere, towards civilization, towards life. He pointed it out to Lydia.

"We must go there," she said.

"Are you still strong enough?"

"I'll make myself!" and she frowned in her determination.

"Off we go then," said Franz, and they both rose to their feet.

8

THEY WALKED, they dragged themselves along, and slowly, very slowly, they made progress. Pebbles rolled under their feet, making them stumble. The baby was heavy, the box was heavy and its jolting over the rough surface jarred Franz's outstretched arms unbearably. The sun sank lower and lower, and the path turned and twisted continually. As it went higher, it became harder to find, and the two children found it difficult to follow the track. Over and over again they came to a dead end and had to go back the way they had come. The air grew cold. A moment ago they had been warm, now they were shivering. The path seemed to be heading for a sort of pass between two peaks.

"Shall we go on?" Franz asked.

"Yes, we must go at least that far," Lydia said abruptly.

"But suppose we don't get there till nightfall?"

"There may be a village behind there somewhere."

Franz dared not destroy the illusion that kept her going, though he had lost all hope himself. There could not possibly be a village at that height, where nothing, not even a tree, grew, nothing but sparse dried grass. They went on walking, gradually working forward. Now the sun lit only the snowy summits that were glowing red. The baby was crying. Lydia's back was uncomfortable; he was hungry and probably cold.

They tried to hide from each other the despair that increased with every step.

They finally reached the pass, and discovered it to be a narrow plateau. There was no village. They marched on like sleepwalkers, and neither spoke.

They came to the edge of the plateau and saw before them an amphitheatre, a vast amphitheatre of mountain peaks, jagged and sharp-pointed like those they had left behind. The path went on, however, tumbling down into a deep valley filled with mist as evening drew on. The children, worn out, tried to peer down into the valley depths.

"I can see a village!" Lydia shouted.

"Where?"

"Down there," and she pointed to a space at the end of the winding trail. Her face was at once transformed, her cheeks were flushed, and her eyes were filled with hope.

"You sit down and rest here for a while," said Franz, "while I go to see how far away it is."

"But, Franz, it's not as far as the way we've come — you don't expect us to sleep out tonight, do you? We're so high up, it will be too cold."

"I'd rather go and see. When I signal to you that it's all right, then you can come and join me."

"I want to go with you, I don't want to stay here alone." She stumbled as she spoke, and caught Franz's arm.

"That's just plain nonsense," he said firmly. "You simply must rest, and I'll signal as soon as I possibly can."

She recognized the sudden authority in his voice, and gave in.

64

Sitting on a boulder by the side of the road she watched him go, as she gave the baby his second feed. The silence was frightening as the small sound of Franz's footsteps died away. The last rosy glow faded from the last gilded peak, and it was suddenly very cold.

She watched Franz's figure dwindle to a small shape scarcely visible on the mountain track.

Lydia's hopes were fixed on the village set out there like a toy. Her heart beat fast. Franz must be quite near now, he should be signaling. Why wasn't he waving to her as he had promised? What was happening?

The baby finished his bottle and fell asleep. Lydia put him down carefully on her coat, which she had spread out on the ground, and walked forward a few yards, shielding her eyes with her hand. Franz's outline was bigger, he was coming back. What on earth was he doing? He was coming back, running a few yards, then stopping as if he was exhausted, then starting again. Lydia dared not think, nor try to understand. She waited, still and frozen.

When he was within earshot she called, "Franz!" and then again, "Franz!"

He raised his hand, made a vague gesture with his arms, and walked on, but more slowly now as though he were at the end of his strength. She ran towards him and flung herself on him.

"Franz, why have you come back? Why didn't you signal to me?"

"Lydia —"

"Isn't it a village?"

"Yes — it's a village."

"Then what's wrong, Franz?"

"It's empty," he said, so low she could scarcely hear him. "It's a deserted village, like the other one. I was afraid it would be," he added, forcing himself to speak. "That's why I didn't want you to come."

His voice roughened suddenly with the tears he would not shed. And then they both broke down. Lydia was the first to recover. She took Franz by the hand and said in a small voice, sounding her last hope, "Let's go back to the house. Let's go back to our house."

"Yes," he said, squeezing her hand as hard as he could, "that's all we've got. Let's go back to our house."

9

IT WAS very dark and very cold. They had been walking so long they were afraid they must be lost, but they could not bring themselves to talk about it. Franz's leg was hurting him; Lydia's feet were blistered and the sleeping child on her back had become so heavy that she felt as though she were bent in two. Franz's hand was bleeding where the belt pulling the box had cut into it. Lydia was crying.

Only their longing to get back to their house kept them on their feet and gave them strength to go on walking. From time to time Lydia sat down, exhausted, in the pitch blackness that surrounded them. Mechanically they retraced their steps along the path that was so hard to follow. The baby, awake now, did not cry. He seemed to understand that this was an ordeal he must share with them.

At last Franz spoke, and his voice was almost a whisper, "Lydia! I can hear the stream!"

"Can you?"

"Yes, I can hear it very faintly. Listen!"

There it was singing away, suddenly familiar, like a lullaby, or the voice of a friend.

"Are you sure it's *our* stream?"

"Of course I am — there wasn't another on our way out. And we can't have gone all that far astray!"

Led by the sound, they came to the stream. They were walking very slowly now, afraid of falling down exhausted at every step.

"Franz," said Lydia. "Here's the stairway."

"We're nearly home," he gasped.

"I just can't climb up."

"I'll go first, take my hand!"

"My legs are quite dead."

"A few more minutes, and we'll be at the house."

"Can you see it?"

"Yes, there it is! We're nearly at the garden."

"Are there still many steps?"

"Only two, hang on to me, don't give up now. There, we're home!"

There was no moon, the garden was a black lake, the house a shapeless mass. The icy breath of the mountain soaked the grass and froze their feet in their dusty shoes. They reached the door, and heard with joy the familiar creaking as it opened and they went in. Franz fumbled to light the candle. It blinded them, but it revived them too. The flowers that Lydia had picked the day before were blooming in the old jar on the table. The bed with its thick blankets promised warmth and sleep. A faint smell of chocolate and warm milk hung in the air from their breakfast.

Lydia put the baby in his carry-cot; he looked at her in silence, and as though he were frightened. Once in his cot, he seemed to relax. She kissed him, and he closed his eyes.

Exhausted, Lydia fell onto the bed. Franz sat down beside her and put his arm around her shoulders. She leaned

her head against him, and tears fell slowly down her haggard little face. They sat in silence, overcome by despair.

Gradually a feeling of peace stole over them, almost of well-being. Everything was just as it had been the day before; the door and shutter closed, the table with its flowers, the bed, the sleeping baby, the candlelight.

"Don't cry," said Franz. "We're snug enough here, this will be our house, our home. Tomorrow we'll fix everything up as best we can, and we'll just wait until something happens. We're lucky that there's two of us ... think what it would be like alone ... if you weren't here, I couldn't bear it."

"If you weren't here, I'd be dead already," she said.

"But here we are, both of us. So there it is. Now I'm going to light the stove and heat some milk, the way we did this morning. Tomorrow we'll get ourselves organized."

"Yes, of course," she said, drying her eyes and stumbling to her feet. "Tomorrow we'll get ourselves organized."

10

THE FOLLOWING day was another day of sunshine. The sun rose early and one of its rays filtered through a crack in the shutter to play first on the baby's cheek, then on Lydia's hair spread out around her, and next on Franz's eyelids to wake him. Everything was peaceful and quiet in the room. On the table, the remains of their supper made a cozy sort of untidiness, just as it had been left the night before.

Franz sat up, ran his hands through his hair, and felt strong enough for anything. He was the oldest of the three of them, and a boy, so he must play the man's part — the baby was far too young. It was Franz's job to protect and look after the girl and the baby. He remembered Lydia's energy all through the hard time they had had. She would be a great help. So they could wait to see what happened, and not be too unhappy.

He got up quietly, put the dishes into the cooking pot, then went down the stairway, listening to the birds singing. The mauve flowers, half opened, were lazily facing the day. A shaft of sunlight, still rosy with dawn, pierced through the firs.

This was all known and familiar, and to find it again

after having believed it lost, was a comfort. As he climbed up again, he was singing with the birds because he was so happy. Words came into his mind, and the melody with them, out of the strange darkness of his lost memory, perhaps because they somehow belonged to the beauty of the morning:

> *"Give to me the life I love,*
> *Let the lave go by me,*
> *Give the jolly heaven above*
> *And the by-way nigh me.*
> *Bed in the bush with stars to see —*
> *Bread I dip in the river —*
> *There's the life for a man like me,*
> *There's the life for ever."*

As he reached the garden, he saw Lydia coming out of the house.

"Hello!" he yelled, waving his arms.

She put up a hand to shield her eyes, for the light blinded her.

"Hello!" she called back, running towards him. "Hello, did you sleep well?"

"Marvelously! What a wonderful day it is!"

"Yes, I'm madly happy!"

"So am I!"

She laughed, shook out her hair in the sun, and ran off.

"I'm going to wash, I'll be back soon."

"Is the baby asleep?"

"Yes."

Her voice was lost among the trees, and Franz took up his song again:

> *"There's the life for a man like me,*
> *There's the life for ever."*

He went into the house. It was flooded with sunlight pouring in through the open shutter. Lydia had already made the bed and set the table. The rusks and the butter were there, and water was heating on the camp stove. Only the dishes that Franz had brought back with him were missing. He put out the bowls and the mugs, with two spoons and two knives, and then turned down the flame of the stove.

When Lydia came back, she heated the milk and chocolate, and they had breakfast, sitting opposite each other.

"I'm starving!" said Franz.

"Me too, it's terrible!"

"No, it's good."

"But we mustn't eat everything we've got."

"Don't worry. For one thing, I'll go back to the Alpine hut and bring more food and everything else I can lay hands on. For another, I'm sure people can always get by if they've got guts. You'll see."

"You're wonderful," she said.

"No, but I'm happy!"

"I am too, isn't it extraordinary?"

"It isn't extraordinary, it's . . . simply . . . marvelous!" He laughed and clapped his hands together, pushing his bowl away.

"Well, I'm off! I'll probably be gone quite a while, but don't panic!"

"What about your leg?"

"I don't know . . . I think it's better."

"Let me see."

Franz unwound the bandage and Lydia examined the gash very carefully.

"Yes, I do really believe it's healing," she said, with a competent air. "Does it still hurt?"

73

"Oh, only a very little."

"And if I press it here?"

"No, it hardly hurts at all."

"That's a good sign, and it isn't inflamed; it's very clean. Look, I'll put another bandage on, as a protection."

"Where did you learn how to bandage? You do it so well."

"I don't know. Perhaps I . . . no, I don't know any more!"

"That's like me. Just now, coming back from the stream, I found myself singing a song that came from I don't know where. Yet I knew it all right and I think I used to sing it or hear it sung often. Don't let's think of all that, though," he added, shaking his head. "Just for now we must concentrate on getting ourselves organized. Later, we'll see."

"Perhaps something in our heads will suddenly clear up."

"Perhaps. I'll go now so as to have plenty of time to get things done."

"Will you be back for lunch?"

"I don't know."

"It would be exhausting to come back and then set out again; you'd better stay there and do all that you can and then come back before night. I'll give you some buttered biscuits and some chocolate to take with you. Then when you get hungry you can eat them."

"But won't you get fed up on your own?"

"I've lots to do, and there's the baby."

"But . . . you won't be too frightened?"

"I was much more frightened yesterday, and yet I stuck it out, didn't I? I've got to get used to it. Take your coat with you. It may be cold when you come back."

"You think of everything," Franz said.

He hesitated. Lydia was burrowing in the cupboard where, two days before, she had found the dishes.

74

"There!" she said. "I've found a bottle — wash it in the stream as you go by, and fill it with water."

"Oh, thank you. I'll have a fine lunch!"

He picked up his coat and put into his pocket the package of biscuits and chocolate that Lydia had ready for him. He went quietly over to the sleeping baby and looked down at him, then he made for the door.

"I'll come with you to the end of the garden," Lydia said.

"Oh, good."

The sun had already soaked up the dew and warmed the straggling weeds. A wonderful smell rose from the earth and drifted down from the branches of the firs.

Lydia went as far as the steps.

"Goodbye, see you later!"

"See you this evening," she said. "Take your time, don't get too tired. I'll be all right."

"Good."

She walked backwards a few steps.

"I don't like leaving you," he said suddenly.

For answer, Lydia waved her hand gaily. He smiled, and disappeared.

Once she was alone, Lydia experienced the same feeling of despair of that first day, but now it was not nearly so strong. The house itself, solid, secure, protective, had a reassuring air about it. Last night's trial of strength, that agonizing and disappointing trek into the unknown, had proved just how much this shelter, that so luckily had come their way, meant to them.

In the clear morning light it looked so welcoming, with its low eaves and its little window. The wild rose had opened all its buds to the sun, small blue flowers framed the two stone steps before the door, and grass was growing in a friendly sort of way through the cracks. And inside was the warm bed, the table, that had already almost become a family table, the mugs and the spoons, the jar filled with branches of yellow blossoms, lilac bells, and feathery leaves, with which she had decorated the room to give Franz a happy surprise. When they had wanted to leave all this the day before, they were going against the very Providence that had set this house down in their path. From this moment it would be *their* house, and they must arrange everything so that they could live here, and wait.

Resolutely, Lydia refused to think of anything that did not lead to immediate action. She busied herself with the baby, who had just wakened. She undressed him and bathed him with great care in the sunshine, so that he wouldn't catch cold. It was fun to dress him in the baby clothes she had chosen from those in the bag found in the carry-cot the day before. He looked so sweet, all clean and fresh, with his black hair and his lively black almond-shaped eyes. His small face was pale. The terrible day they had spent yesterday had been just as exhausting for him as for Franz and Lydia. But from now on he would have a regular routine, with plenty of sleep, and he would soon be quite fit again.

He was completely happy, staring solemnly at Lydia. While she gave him his bottle, he wriggled his small toes and opened and shut his tiny hands.

"We'll have to choose a name for him," Lydia thought. "We don't know what he's called, and he's not wearing a locket or a name bracelet."

She tried to think of a name, but her mind was quite blank.

"I'll wait until Franz comes back," she decided.

The thought of Franz's return filled her with a sudden

happiness. She put the baby into the box that served him as a cradle, pushed it near the door through which the sun was streaming, and began to put the stove, the dishes, and the food left from breakfast back in the cupboard. As she did so, she sang the song Franz had sung on his way back from the stream, and she felt light-hearted in a way she could neither explain nor understand.

11

WHEN EVERYTHING had been done, the sun was still high in the sky, and Lydia faced the dreary prospect of long hours stretching ahead before Franz came home. She wondered what she could do. The baby was dressed, and he had had his bottle. He was sleeping now, and she must not disturb him. It would be sensible to eat something herself. It must be about midday, and they had had breakfast early. She didn't feel hungry, perhaps because Franz wasn't there. Still, she must eat, if only because she must keep well.

She could not bring herself to set the table. It would be too lonely to eat there by herself. She sat in the sun on the warm doorstep, leaning against the sweetbriar bushes that scented the air, and she made herself eat some buttered biscuits and some chocolate.

"Perhaps Franz is eating his lunch now, at this very moment."

She refused to give way to the anxiety that seized her when she thought of Franz all alone, as she was, in this unknown place. Her eyes closed and she forced herself to think only of the scent of the briar and the warmth of the sun on her cheek. For a little while she slept. It did her good, but when she woke up she saw that the sun's position hadn't changed very much, and there was still a great deal of time to fill in before nightfall. Despair rushed back, blacker than it had been earlier. Her short sleep had made her feel heavy. Was she really awake or was she dreaming? Suppose all this were just a dream? She stood up in an attempt to throw off this feeling, wandered off a little way, and came upon a sort of shed. She went in and looked around, and when she came out she was carrying a number of things which she took into the house. Then she thought: "I'll pick the baby up, he's slept long enough. We'll go for a walk. We'll go to see the village."

The child slept on, unaware of the doubts and dangers that surrounded him. Lydia lifted his hand and opened it by slipping her finger into his smaller ones and then shook it gently, but he did not stir. So she lifted him up and spoke to him.

"Cuckoo! . . . baby! Wake up, my littlest one!"

He opened his eyes and seemed to know her, for he smiled at her immediately. She picked him up in her arms, took his carrying cloak just in case and went out, closing the door behind her.

It was all very pleasant until they went beyond the stream. The baby gurgled and made wild attempts to play with Lydia's hair. But when the deserted and grass-grown street came into view at the end of the path, it looked so sinister that Lydia was frightened. The harsh light of the afternoon blazed down and heightened its air of desolation. Lydia stopped and looked around for something reassuring. There on the left she saw the church on whose steps she had sunk exhausted two days ago. She walked up to it. The door was shut, but when she looked more closely she saw a wooden latch, half eaten away, that lifted easily. She pushed the door open. A gust of damp coldness came to meet her. She put the baby's cloak over her shoulders, with one fold over the child, and went quietly in. There were no pews, only a few dusty chairs. Lydia sat down.

It was a very small church, with a low vaulted roof painted to look like a blue sky, sown with stars, but the paint was peeling off in shreds. A flat circular step led to the chancel. The altar rails seemed to have come loose and the little gate hung open. The wooden altar had hardly any gilding left, but there was some on the lamb that lay there, bearing a cross. There was no altar cloth, no curtain at the tabernacle, no flowers in the two faded vases that stood one on each side.

"I'll bring some," Lydia decided. "Those big daisies in the garden would look fine in those vases." There were still half-burned candles in the candlesticks. On the left of the chancel a saint in carved wood, the paint scaling off, held the folds of her robe with one hand and, smiling, lifted a finger of the other. On the right, a St. Christopher carrying on his shoulder an infant Jesus with a crumbling nose, looked as if he were marching stoutly beneath a veil of cobwebs.

Such silence . . .

Lydia put her feet on the worm-eaten rail of the chair and sat very still, hugging the baby to her, just as though the door on the left were going to open, and a choirboy with his hands joined and a priest with his head bowed over his chalice were going to come through it. Perhaps her despair grew less because of this unconscious expectation. A feeling of infinite peace came upon her, a great calm, and the awareness of a mysterious protection. Was

it because of the mighty angel's wing soaring above her head in the curve of the pointed arch?

The stained-glass window facing her above the tabernacle was all lit up. The sun had just reached it, and the blue mantle of St. Joseph, who held a lily, took on the color of a summer sky, while the scarlet robe of the high priest sparkled like ripe red currants. The Virgin Mary, leaning over her child, gleamed like a honeycomb in her golden gown.

As the sun shone through the stained-glass window, a great chirruping of birds broke out around the leafy branch of a tree that had thrust itself through the window on the left, where no glass remained. The chancel was filled with a sudden gaiety. A bird flew in, darted across like an arrow, and out through a window on the right. Another followed, then returned with a shrill clamor. The air was filled with the whirring of joyous wings. The baby began chuckling and Lydia was so delighted she forgot her sadness. She did not know how long she stayed there. The ancient clock above the porch had stopped long ago at five past twelve. She had fallen into a half sleep and she was drowsily happy, because the stained-glass window above her head was lit up, because the sun was also streaming in through the window on the right, sending a rosy glow over the gilded lamb on the altar and over the saint with her uplifted finger.

"She looks as though she wants to tell a secret," Lydia thought, "— as though she were saying 'Listen!' "

When the rosy sunbeams withdrew from the chancel and were no more than a stain on the crumbling walls, Lydia stood up. The birds had gone. She felt that it would be wise to follow their example, and to avoid being overtaken by nightfall while she was still on the road. The baby had fallen asleep on the nearby chair where she had put him, to ease her aching arms.

She picked him up, wrapped him warmly in his cloak, sent a kiss to the saint carved in scaling wood, genuflected in front of the altar, and went on her way.

12

Night came on with stealthy slowness. The sun had completely disappeared some time ago, and now a grayish light was spreading over the open spaces. Black shadows filled the hollows of the rocks beneath the trees, and the air had turned damp and cold. Franz felt his hands grow numb, and he shivered. Only then did he realize that he had stayed too late, and that he might lose his way back to the house. He began to worry about Lydia's anxiety if he were not back before nightfall.

Working feverishly, he gathered together the things he had sorted out and tied up, and piled them into a packing-case emptied for the purpose. He found a stout rope that would be better than his belt for dragging the box along, and fixed it securely with a firm knot. It would do very well, and Lydia had been right when she said, that morning, "We will have to take care of our clothes. We don't know how long we'll have to make them last." It was obvious that his nice leather belt wouldn't have lasted long if he'd gone on hauling packing-cases with it.

Franz set out. It was darker now. Two evenings before,

returning along this same path, he had expected to spend the night out of doors. He had not known that Lydia had found a house. Yesterday they had been like shipwrecked sailors, miserable and lost, worn-out with wandering. To-night, although he was tired, he had a deep feeling of satisfaction that he was making for a definite place where he could be sure of shelter and rest. There was pleasure, after the long day's solitude, in the thought of seeing Lydia and the baby again, and he hurried on, in spite of the weight of the case, which dragged painfully at the muscles of his arms and neck. Actually, he had been thinking of the other two all day long. Every single thing he had found in that narrow hut he had chosen for one of them.

"That will be for Lydia, and that for the little one," he had said, and then suddenly thought, "How odd, we don't know what he's called. We'll have to give him a name; we'll do it later, when I'm back with Lydia, after we've eaten."

When he came to the beginning of the sinister village, it looked still more ominous in the pale light of the moon. He felt at the end of his strength, but everything looked so threatening that he automatically quickened his step. The shadows of the tumbledown houses stretched out along the street, and the dark branches of the trees above the roofs waved in the breeze. Franz suddenly remembered a story about witches that someone had told him when he was very small . . . remembering it was a glimmer in his shuttered mind . . . the story of a witch. She used to run into a clearing by moonlight, waving dark branches, and then she would mount her broomstick, rise above the forest, and go shrieking into space, in search of children who had been naughty. Who had told him the story? . . . a very old woman wearing a white apron. Who was she? . . . her name was on the tip of his tongue.

"Lisel!" He shouted it in a harsh voice that seemed torn out of him.

The word ran around the high mountains and its icy echo came back to him. "Lisel-el-el . . . Lisel-el-el- . . ."

For a moment he had an awareness of infinite gentleness, and he felt as though his mind were opening to the light. Then darkness enfolded him once more and he was back among the ruined houses where the dark branches rustled against each other.

By now Franz was at the end of the village, and he found that he was shaking and his brow was damp with sweat. But as he drew near the church, the bell moved gently in the wind, and the sound of it was like the voice of a friend. Immediately afterwards he heard the rushing of the stream. The wind died down among the trees, and Franz grew warm as he hauled the case up step by step. Luckily he found a way of getting it up to the garden by pushing from underneath, and rolling it over like a barrel. Up there the wind was stronger than in the village. It seemed to flow like an air current through the opening of the valley, then turn and go off again like an arrow, icy and stinging, through the other end. The tall grasses bowed beneath the rhythm of its prolonged howling. It was frightening, and so desolate that Franz shivered, even though he was hot after dragging the packing-case. He saw the house at that very moment. The window was a golden rectangle in the dark, for inside the candles were lit, and the same golden rectangle shone on the moving grasses, friendly and comforting. The house held the promise of life, of warmth and light. Two people he could not do without were in there, and they could not do without him. They were waiting for him.

"Hello there!" he shouted. "Hello!"

The door opened immediately.

"Franz!"

"Lydia!"

He began to run, pulling the heavy box after him without even feeling its weight. Lydia ran out to meet him. Together they went into the house, and hugged each other as though they had been parted for years.

13

ONCE THE door was closed, the wind and the cold and the crowding ghosts all stayed outside. The room with its flowers and its candlelight seemed like paradise to Franz. Lydia had put the baby to bed and set the table. She knelt on the floor as Franz fumbled with the rope around the box, eager to show her his treasure-trove.

"It's so nice, our home," he said, looking around. His fair hair, rumpled by the wind, stood out around his face, which glowed with pleasure.

"Do you think it's all right? Look, I put the jar of flowers on the chimney-piece opposite the candle, when I set the table."

"It looks fine," Franz said. "You do it all so well."

"When we get more things it will look even better. What have you brought?"

"Heaps of things. The box is full to the brim."

"Oh, this is fun!" she said, clapping her hands. "Show me, quickly!"

While he was untying the rope, she looked at his hands, a boy's hands, square and sturdy. Franz saw her watching and suddenly stopped what he was doing.

"Oh! how dirty my hands are! I should have washed as I came by the stream," he said, "but I was in such a hurry to get back."

"Don't worry — I've something to show you —" Lydia was laughing. "I've been working too! Come and see — do come and see!"

At the end of the room, hidden by the bulk of the big wooden cupboard, there was a small door in the wall. She opened it, then went to fetch a candle. Holding it high, she said triumphantly, "There! What do you think of our bathroom?"

Franz looked into a store-room that must once have contained wood, and animals too, for wisps of hay lingered in the corners in spite of Lydia's cleaning. The ceiling sloped down and the thatched roof could be seen between two stout beams. A rough window showed up against the dark. A large wooden tub stood on the floor against the wall. Beside it was a tall pitcher with copper bands, filled with water, and a piece of soap lying on a green leaf. Two towels were hanging from the beams overhead.

Franz was struck dumb with astonishment and admiration.

"It's very grand, isn't it, our bathroom?"

"It's wonderful! Where on earth did you find all this?"

"Well, it was so sunny after lunch that we went into the field behind the house. I saw a shed up there, and I looked inside. I'll show you tomorrow. I found this tub and then this lovely pitcher. They were terribly dirty, so I washed them in the stream. And since I'd already discovered this room earlier, I suddenly thought how marvelous it would be to wash in. We won't have to go down to the stream and, after all, when winter comes it will be impossible to go outside."

Franz noticed that she spoke quite casually and without any distress of spending the winter there, and without knowing why, he felt glad about it.

"What about the towels, Lydia, and the soap? Were they in the shed, too?"

"Oh no. All that was in the box you brought back the day before yesterday."

Franz washed his hands with great enjoyment. When he had finished he emptied the tub through a door which led outside, and then put it back in its place.

"What else did you do?" he asked.

"We went down to the village, but that deserted street was so sad I felt frightened. And then just as I was looking around I saw the church. Do you remember that church? I sat down on the steps there, that first day I was so tired."

"Oh yes, I remember," Franz said. "What did you do then?"

"Well, I felt I wanted to go in, as if someone were inviting me. Franz, it's so beautiful. There's a gilded lamb on the altar and there are still bits of wax candle in the candlesticks. There's a lovely stained-glass window, and a saint lifting her finger as though she were going to speak and a St. Christopher — he's dreadfully dirty and all covered with dust. We'll go and clean him up, won't we? And we'll take some of those big flowers from the garden. There are still two vases on the altar."

"Of course we will," said Franz. "We'll go and put it all in order. That poor church! Just now as I came past, the bell sounded and it was such a cheerful noise. Perhaps it was telling me that you had been there."

Franz began taking the things out of the box, one by one, and piling them on the table.

"There's heaps of food. I found more canned stuff and I

brought a lot of it back. Here it is — sardines, more sardines, and still more sardines — at least ten cans. And tuna fish — here's some ham. And these are green beans — one, two, three, four, five cans. There are lots more. I couldn't bring them all back because the box gets heavy so quickly. And I found some more boxes of candles, thank goodness."

"So did I," she said. "Huge yellow candles."

"Those are wax candles, we mustn't use them up too fast. We'll only light up when it's really dark, and we'll go to bed early."

"Do you know, Franz, I found a drawer full of clothes in the cupboard. Look at this thick cape. There are jackets, sweaters, and two pairs of denim trousers and two of corduroy. There aren't any girl's clothes so I'll just have to make do with these. They're too big, but I've found a sewing box. Franz —" she asked, "can I go to the hut with you tomorrow?"

"It's too far."

"But I'm not so tired now."

"We'd have to take the baby. I could carry him on the way there, but I'd be too loaded on the way back."

Lydia gave the matter some thought.

"Franz, I've got an idea! When we want to go out together, we'll put him in the box, as if it were a carriage, and we'll pull him along with the rope. We'll put his carrycot inside, so that he'll be comfortable."

"I'd much rather we were all together, you know that," he said. "The day seems long when I'm on my own. You could wait for me half way."

"Listen!" said Lydia. "He's talking to us!"

The baby, now awake, was chattering away. Quite a speech, no doubt, if they had been able to understand it. He punctuated it with shouts of triumph as he waved his arms and legs in the air. Lydia took a spoon from the table and held it out to him.

"Here's something to play with, little dear one," she said. "Isn't it pretty? See how it shines!"

The baby took the spoon and tried to put it in his mouth.

"Let's find a name for him," said Franz, coming across to look at the baby with her.

"Don't you think he's a bit Chinese? His skin is dark and he's so tiny. And his eyes are black and slanting."

"He has hardly any nose," Franz said.

"Wait a minute . . ."

Just then the baby, looking at the two faces leaning over him, began chattering again, enjoying the unintelligible sounds he made.

"Ta-o-ta-ta-o-ta . . ."

"There you are!" said Franz. "That's his name! We'll call him Tao; it sounds like a Chinese name."

The baby looked at them with his narrow slanting eyes, then threw the spoon Lydia had given him on the floor.

"All right, we'll call you Tao," she said to him. "It's a very pretty name."

She left him with his new plaything, and opened the big cupboard. Franz brought the supplies over to her.

"Pass them up to me," said Lydia, climbing onto a stool.

There was a tremendous satisfaction in getting themselves settled in, and making a home for themselves, after the exhaustion, the sense of being lost and defenceless, the cold and the dark of the preceding nights. There was no longer any question of leaving the house, only of waiting until something happened, as it surely would.

"Anything else to go in?" she asked.

"No, I've given you everything. I'll just put the box away for tomorrow and then we'll eat. *Ich habe einen Wolfshunger.*"

"What?"

"*Einen Wolfshunger habe ich, und Du?*"

"What did you say?"

"*Ich sage Dir, ich habe einen Hunger!*"

"But — I can't understand what you're saying!"

"*Was? Wie bitte?*"

"You're saying words I don't understand." Lydia's eyes were anxious as she stared at Franz.

He stopped laughing, began to say, "*Verstehst Du nicht?*" . . . and fell silent. His eyes too were anxious. He rubbed his hand across his brow, murmured several more words that were unintelligible to Lydia, shook his head, sighed deeply.

"I said that I was hungry!"

"Ah! Now I can understand again!" and she too heaved a sigh, as though relieved of her anxiety. "What on earth was the matter with you? Were you trying to make me laugh? You only frightened me!"

"No," Franz said. "I wasn't trying to make you laugh or to frighten you. I simply said I was hungry, that's all. You're the one who scared me. You don't feel sick?"

"No, of course not."

"You feel all right?"

"Perfectly all right."

"Well then, it's nothing. I don't know what happened . . ."

"I don't either. I haven't a clue."

"We haven't a clue about anything just now, have we? Anyway, there's no sense in getting worked up about it. It's over now."

They ate their meal quickly, for they were very sleepy. Lydia occasionally fell silent and looked closely at Franz. It seemed to her now that he didn't speak quite the same

94

way as she did. He had a sort of accent that was a little different ... but she was too tired to think of it just then. She fell asleep on a corner of the table. Franz had to shake her to wake her up, and almost carry her to bed. They fell into it fully dressed, and dropped at once into a sound sleep.

14

Days and weeks went by quickly. They grew accustomed to their new life, which fell into an orderly pattern. Every evening the sun disappeared sooner behind the mountains and every evening Franz returned a little earlier. He had found a number of precious things: more food, some blankets, and several books. Exploratory trips in all directions had firmly convinced him that they could not get safely out of the mountains, and they were making the little house more and more their home. Autumn was on its way. The tall pines would stay green, but the leafy trees scattered here and there, the birches, and a few scanty bushes were turning rust red, golden yellow or purple brown. Some of the leaves were so beautiful that Lydia broke off whole branches and arranged them in jars, to decorate the house. Franz selected specimens to press between the pages of a book. These books were for grown-ups, intended to while away the time for Alpine climbers when they were snowed up, perhaps for two or three days, in the hut.

"Never mind," said Franz. "We'll read them just the same. They'll teach us all sorts of things."

That very evening, as it happened, he planned to go back even earlier, for he wanted to make a bookshelf to stand them on, so he was hurrying home.

For two days now the weather had not been so fine as when they first set up house; the sun was often over-clouded, and an icy wind bent the grasses and shook the bushes. Today Franz found himself shivering, even though he was dragging a heavy packing-case, and had a blanket and two cushions over his shoulders. As he gazed into the sky between the high mountains he saw a flock of birds go by with outstretched wings. He wondered where they were going and what country lay beyond that barrier, what the birds could see while they were so high up, what horizon, or plain, or sea perhaps...

If a plane ever came that way, all three of them, Lydia, the baby and himself, would fly up and they too would see the plains and the sea. They might even recognize their own country. Then their memory would come back to them and they would at last find out what had happened to them... all at once a lump came into his throat, and his eyes filled with tears.

The birds were gone, the sky grew dark, it became still colder. He felt so alone, so trapped, so small in that wild place that he began to run, in spite of the weight he was pulling behind him, towards Lydia, towards Tao, towards home.

"But a plane would only stop if it knew we were here," — the thought came all at once into his mind. "There'd have to be some sort of signal... there should be a flag ...tomorrow I'll set up a flagpole. I'll look for a long enough branch, and I'll fix a sheet to it for a signal."

When he reached home, Lydia was making tea.

"I thought you'd be cold when you came back, and this should warm us both up. I'm absolutely frozen."

"What a good idea!" he said, pleased.

He sat with the bowl in front of him, rubbing his cold hands. Lydia buttered two rusks and handed them to him.

"I'll take you with me tomorrow," he said as he crunched them up. "D'you know what I'm going to do? I'm going to put up a flagpole and tie a flag to it, so that any plane coming over will see it. I want you to give me something for the flag — this sheet, perhaps."

"Oh no, we need it too badly. There are only three and that's not really enough. Perhaps if we look around we might find some more...we must have enough bed-clothes, especially when it grows colder."

"It must be terribly cold here in these mountains in winter," Franz said.

"Yes, I'd already thought of that. I'm going to cut this sheet in half for Tao. And I'll let him have that thick tartan rug. Then he'll have a real cozy bed, poor darling."

"Yes, you're right, of course, but what shall we use to make the signal for the planes?"

"Do you really think planes will come here?"

"Of course I do, some day."

"Have you seen one?"

"Not so far."

"Do you honestly think a signal could be seen from a plane?"

"Why not?"

A somber silence fell between them. The baby had fallen asleep, clasping in his fist the spoon that was his only plaything.

"Listen," said Franz at last, "it's better on the whole

not to think about it too much. All we can do now is just go on living — do what we can to help and then just wait till it happens, and meanwhile make the best we can with what we've got. I'm going to use those planks we found in the shed to make a shelf for our books. Tomorrow we'll put up the flagpole, and set up an observation post."

"I'll let you have one of the pieces of stuff I found in the cupboard to make a flag. It's very thick sailcloth and it'll stand up to the wind," she said. "You start on the bookshelf — I'll clear the table."

In the shed at the end of the garden, Franz had found an ax, a hammer, and some nails. With a stone he had managed to give the ax a very good edge. Here and there rusty nails were embedded in the crumbling walls. He had drawn them out, straightened them and polished them up by the same means. He must try to save the new ones, everything was so precious. Now the ax would be a very useful tool. With its sharp edge he could cut and plane the old planks. He set to work while Lydia washed up the tea-things in the store-room that was now grandly called "the bathroom."

Daylight was fading. Outside everything was shrouded in a desolate gray mist. Gloomy clouds writhed and twisted down from the mountain peaks. Lydia poked her head through the skylight and shivered. The smell of damp earth mingled with the tangy scent of wet pines. Nowhere was there any friendly light, or any sign of life and nothing at all in the twilight but the mountain slopes fading from view, and the silence, the unbroken silence over all.

Seized with panic, she felt that she must scream. Then from the other room came the sound of Franz's ax, a heartening sound, reminding her that he was there, a sound that brought life into this wilderness, and broke the terror of the silence. Lydia closed the skylight and went in to join him. He raised his head and smiled. Lydia smiled too.

"What's up? You look as pale as death," he said. "Are you cold?"

"Yes, I am," she said. "Aren't you?"

"I must say it isn't very warm!"

She suddenly understood that he felt as she did about their loneliness, the gray day, the bad weather heralded by the icy cold, the threat of a winter of a kind they did not know. She leaned over Tao, touched his hand, and then straightened, her mind made up.

"He's frozen," she said. "I'm going to light a fire."

"What a good idea! Let me help."

Franz began chopping wood with his ax, and soon he had enough to keep a fire going until bedtime. He struck a match. The wood was so dry that a clear crackling flame shot up immediately, and soon a cheerful blaze sent its flickering light all over the room.

Lydia brought the cradle to the hearth and sat down beside it on a stool. With the sewing box she had found, she would be able to alter the trousers and shirts and jackets to fit Franz and herself. If she set to work now, her mood of despair would pass and she wouldn't have time to think about how frightened she was. The fire was already making her feel better. It wasn't only that it warmed the room. There was something friendly about the leaping flames that crackled and spluttered beside her.

Lydia gave her mind to her sewing. She didn't find it very easy. There was not much difficulty in shortening hems, but to take in the width was another thing. Several

100

times she stood up and held the trousers against her, to see whether they would do. But without a mirror it was nearly impossible.

Franz meanwhile had finished making two rough brackets to support the shelf. Since his only tools were an ax, a saw, a knife and a big stone, the only way he could give them rounded edges of a sort was by rubbing them with the stone which was hard and had a very rough surface. He paused for a moment to rest and looked at the fire blazing in the crude fireplace, the baby peacefully asleep, and Lydia sitting wholly absorbed, sewing busily, her blonde hair falling over her work and all but hiding her face.

The frightful cold and seeping dampness, had gone from the room. It was beginning to feel cozy and like Lydia, Franz found himself less despairing and more hopeful. Tomorrow they would set up a flagpole. Obviously planes flew occasionally over these mountains. One of them would see the flag, would land . . . and they would be safe.

"What a marvelous idea it was to light the fire, Lydia."

"Do you like it? It's much brighter, isn't it?"

"Yes, I was feeling a bit low," he confessed. "But I'm on top of the world now!"

As he spoke the house was shaken by a sudden gust of wind. A shower of rain beat down hard on the door and window-pane. Lydia laughed.

"Me too," she said. "I was feeling really blue, but now I'm thinking of other things!"

"Your fire has given us a sense of proportion again," Franz said, brushing his fair hair from his eyes, and he too laughed as another gust shook the little house that stood alone.

101

"Show me what you've done," she said. "Oh, how pretty! How clever you are! How did you do the edges without the proper tools?"

"I don't really know. I scratched away with the knife and rubbed it with the stone, and it sort of happened by itself. I'm going to fix them properly with these nails and then put the shelf up. There, it's as simple as that . . ."

"I'll hold the brackets while you bang the nails in." It took quite a while, but the noise of the hammer knocking in the nails helped to drown the sound of the wind and the rain. Tao was awake but he didn't cry. He had found his spoon and was trying to lift it, chattering away to himself, enjoying his game.

When the bookshelf was finished it looked most handsome, and Franz stepped back to have a good look at it while Lydia put the books in their place.

At once the whole aspect of the room changed. It looked more civilized, more distinguished, more comfortable. Lydia stood back beside Franz.

"It looks fine, doesn't it?"

"It's marvelous!" Franz said.

They suddenly realized that it was dark, and only the fire gave them light.

"How quickly the time's gone. It's already night."

Franz lit two candles.

"I've cut down one pair of trousers to fit me," Lydia said. "I'll wear them with a sweater tomorrow when we make the flagpole. It's beginning to be really cold."

"Yes, trousers will be better to work in. And you could put your dress and your coat away. We must keep them for the day they come to find us."

"D'you think when we leave here we'll remember who we are and where we came from?"

"Of course. Anyway they'll soon tell us, won't they?"

"But —" she said and she looked thoughtful, "would —" Then she stopped short.

"What did you say?"

"Nothing."

"You began to say something."

"No, it's nothing. Tomorrow we'll set up the flagpole. We'll go early. Let's have something to eat now, and go straight to bed afterwards."

"I'll take this wood out, put the tools away, and wash my hands."

"Don't go outside in the rain!"

"Of course not. I'm just going to put the wood in a corner of the bathroom."

He went into the other room, and Lydia heard him singing.

15

ALL NIGHT long, wind and rain beat relentlessly against the house. Once or twice the uproar was so great that Franz and Lydia were wakened.

"What's that, Franz?"

"Don't be frightened. It must be a tree crashing at the end of the garden."

"It's a good thing there aren't any around the house."

"Yes, it is. You see, we really are lucky."

Both times Lydia leaned over what she called the cradle, just beside the bed, to see if Tao was warm enough. But he was sleeping peacefully, snugly tucked in his sheets, beneath the tartan rug folded in four.

Dawn brought silence.

"It's all quiet, the storm's over," Franz said.

He got up and opened the wooden shutter. The wind had died down and it had stopped raining, but the weather was still threatening. Heavy clouds hung low in the early morning sky.

"I can't see the mountains at all!"

"Good!" Lydia said. "I'm frightened of them, specially in the evening."

She picked up the feeding bottle she had put under the mattress to keep warm and gave it to the baby, who opened his eyes.

"I would never have thought of that," said Franz.

"What? Putting the bottle under the mattress?"

"It's still warm!"

"Yes, and it saves using the gasoline. We'll have to make that and the paraffin last as long as possible."

"You're so good at all this, Lydia."

"Not really, not so good as you. And if I am, it's because you show me how."

"In what way?"

"Oh, the way you cope with everything, without ever grumbling about it!"

There was a short silence and then Lydia went to the window.

"The ground is soaked!" she cried out.

"Yes, it will be easy to set up a flagpole."

Lydia clapped her hands. "Quick, quick, let's get ready!"

She was first in the bathroom, and she washed very quickly. The water in the pitcher was freezing. When she had finished, she carefully folded the dress and the petticoat she had been wearing up till now, and put on the trousers she had altered the evening before, with a heavy blue sweater. The sleeves were much too long, so she rolled them up. It was really too big for her, but it was wonderfully warm.

"Oh, this is much more comfortable," she thought with satisfaction. She ran out of the bathroom.

"Franz, do tell me! Do I look all right like this?"

Franz looked at her. She laughed and stretched out her arms to show herself off. Her face was glowing with the icy water she had washed in and her golden hair, brushed

106

and combed, gleamed like the missing sun against the vivid blue of her trousers and sweater.

"You look terrific," he said, "absolutely terrific!"

She was looking around in search of something.

"I wish I had a mirror. I do want to see what my trousers look like."

"They look fine, honestly," Franz said, and added, "but we could do with a mirror." He seemed to be turning the problem over in his mind.

"Go and get washed as quickly as you can," Lydia said. "I'll make breakfast."

"I already have. I went to the stream."

"In this cold weather?"

"Yes — I didn't waste time!"

They did not spend long over breakfast. Franz fixed a rope to one of the boxes he had brought back earlier. Lydia put the covers and the carry-cot inside, and then wrapped Tao warmly in his carrying cloak and laid him carefully in the cot. Then she put the thick brown blanket from the big bed over him.

"I don't think he'll get cold."

"He certainly won't!" said Franz.

"His bottle will keep warm. I've put it under the cushion."

They closed the door of the house securely behind them and set out, Franz hauling the box by the rope. They carried it between them down the steps. Water dripped from the trees that had been soaked in the rain that night, and the steps were so slippery that Franz and Lydia had difficulty keeping on their feet. Tao laughed in imitation, in his own way, and this outburst of children's laughter brought life to the silence of the gray morning. They went past the tree uprooted by the storm. As it fell, it had

107

crushed the smaller trees and bushes in its path. It lay like a huge body on the ground and great splinters from its trunk had been hurled to left and right.

"I've just thought of something," Franz said. "That tree will supply us with wood for a long time. I'll bring the ax tomorrow and chop it up. And I'll take these chunks back to the house now. Wait for me."

Lydia sat down near the stream and talked to Tao.

"See how pretty the rain is on the leaves. It shines like diamonds . . . Look at that bird up there, high in the sky!" And Tao gurgled his reply. All at once Lydia heard something moving near her. It sounded as if an animal caught in the trailing branches of a bush were struggling to get free. Frightened, she rose to her feet, and as she did so, a hen came out of the bush, soaked and rumpled and clucking at the top of her voice. Her cluck! cluck! clucking was so persistent that Lydia burst out laughing. The hen seemed delighted to have discovered a human being in this solitude, and she scratched the ground until she had made a shallow hole. Then she settled herself in it.

Gently Lydia put out a hand to stroke her. The hen, far from being afraid, appeared to enjoy it, nodding her head and murmuring in her throat.

"What on earth's that?" said Franz.

"Franz, it's a hen!"

"So it is," he said as he came up to them. "It really is a hen. Where did it come from?"

"Could it have come from a house we didn't see?"

"We looked everywhere," Franz said. "No, it's not that. I guess it belonged to the owner of our house and it stayed behind when he left."

"Yes, of course, that must be it."

"We could eat it perhaps," said Franz. "It would last us several days."

"What a horrible thing to suggest!" said Lydia. "I don't want to eat her. She's so nice . . . I can stroke her like a cat."

"So you can. She's a nice creature all right, but what are we to do with her?"

"Carry her back to the house."

Franz tried to seize the hen, but she flapped her wings and made a great noise, until she escaped from his hands and ran into the bushes.

"You see!" said Lydia. "She knew you wanted to kill her! I do hope she comes back!"

Franz poked into the bushes with a dry branch, and Lydia called to her, "Hennypenny, dear little Henny, come along. Do come!" But there was no movement.

"Oh well, don't let's waste any more time," Franz said. "We'll come back tomorrow and try to find her. Let's get on to the camp, quick!"

16

EVERYTHING WENT well on the journey. Tao was shaken about a little, but he seemed perfectly willing to accept this method of transportation. The children hurried through the deserted village, for in the horrible gray morning mist it looked even more gaunt and melancholy. They had decided to go back to the place where they had first met, to that barren waste of rock and scrub where Lydia had come upon Franz nearly unconscious on the ground, where they had found Tao, where they had slept among the roots of a tree-trunk. They planned to make what they were already calling their observation post, on that spot. They set to work as soon as they reached it. First they had to choose the site for their flagpole, then look for the pole itself. Lydia soon found a pine completely stripped, and she led Franz to it. It was still standing, but it had lost all its branches, and its tall black trunk rose in solitary splendor to the sky.

"There's the best pole," she said. "It'll be much stronger than any we could make."

Franz agreed and, grasping the trunk, he climbed to

the top, using the few remaining stumps of branches for foothold. From below Lydia watched anxiously.

"If you hear it creaking, please come down at once, Franz."

"It's as safe as houses," he assured her from his perch.

"You're sure it will hold?"

"What?"

"That branch your foot is on."

"Yes, of course!"

Franz fastened the piece of coarse cotton as well as he could with part of the rope he had used to drag Tao's box.

"Make sure it's fast," Lydia shouted.

"Can you see it?" he called, leaning to look down at her.

"Yes, it's fine. It's flapping about like a real flag!"

Franz shinned down the tree and stood back to admire his handiwork from below.

"Not bad at all. But . . . I've just thought of something."

"What?"

"I think I'd better put up a signpost too."

"How?"

"You'll see."

He had brought his tools with him, as well as a piece of wood, which he had planed until it was smooth and glossy. He piled some twigs together and set light to them. As soon as they were charred through, he scored the word HELP in huge letters on the wood, and drew an arrow that pointed in the direction of the village. Then he nailed the board to the tree.

"So anyone who comes along will see that we need help and will come to look for us," he explained to Lydia, who had been watching in silent admiration.

"The rain may wash the letters away."

"I'll write them again."

111

They stood a long time looking at their work, without speaking, until Lydia said, "Someone's sure to come, aren't they?"

"Of course!"

But deep inside, Franz was far less certain of it than he appeared to be.

They had their lunch of sardines and buttered rusks, and drank the water they had brought with them in the bottle.

"All the same," Lydia said, crunching her last rusk, "now it's getting colder, we must have proper meals. I'll open one of the cans of vegetables tonight. I can heat them on the camp stove."

"Better do it over the fire, so that we can save on the gasoline."

"Yes, of course. In the fireplace over our wood fire. There's a hook there to hang the pot on."

"That'll be fine," Franz said. It would be good to have a hot meal, a real meal.

Meanwhile, however, rain threatened and the sky grew overcast. It was easy to see that it would soon be dark. The damp went straight through their clothes, and the children, poorly fed, shivered with cold.

"What do we do now?" Lydia asked.

"Let's go back. I'm afraid of getting caught in a storm."

They set out on the path back to the village. Tao was sleeping. Just before they came to the bend they passed the tree that had sheltered them that first night.

"Remember?" Franz said.

"Yes. We're much better off now."

"That's the way to look at it," he said. "You're so right, Lydia. We'll always be able to be content with what we have by thinking how much worse it could be!"

And like the night when shaking with fear, she had come to find him, they held hands and began to sing to chase the ghosts away.

On their stone doorstep between the two wild rose trees, lay a dark mass.

"Look, Franz!"

"What?"

"There's something on the doorstep."

"Wait here with Tao, I'll go and see."

He went to investigate and burst out laughing. Cupping his hands to his mouth, he shouted, "Guess what?"

"I don't know."

"It's the hen we saw this morning. Come and see!"

"The hen!"

Lydia took Tao into her arms and ran. The hen blearily opened her eyes and puffed up her feathers.

"Is she sick?"

"Not in the least, she's asleep. It's her bedtime!"

"Let me take her. I'll put her in the shed at the end of the garden."

"Then give me the baby."

Lydia handed Tao over, and gently lifted the hen, who made no objection. Together they brought her to the shed.

She seemed to know where she was for she perched at once on an old wheelbarrow and seemed ready to settle down to sleep again.

"You were right," said Lydia. "She certainly lived here before."

"Animals don't like to be on their own," Franz said. "It's because we're here that she's come back."

"What luck! Oh, Franz, it makes us less alone too."

"It's something else alive," he said thoughtfully.

They both stroked her and Lydia even kissed her on her

113

soft downy head. They went off happily to the house. Franz brought in the cushion and the covers that had been wrapped around Tao. Then they shut the door securely and lit the fire which burned up more quickly than the day before because the hearth was still warm. Franz opened a can of vegetables and Lydia put them in the cooking pot with a lump of butter. Then they hung the pot over the crackling flames that gave off a fine resinous smell. Franz lit a candle, and while Lydia attended to Tao, he sat reading by the fire.

The following morning when day had scarcely dawned and they were still asleep, a triumphant cockadoodledoo sounded under their window. Lydia opened her eyes, but she was so heavy with sleep that she closed them again immediately. A second crow, an even louder clarion call, echoed and re-echoed through the mountains, then a third and a fourth, as the sun appeared in a hollow between two peaks. The light filtered through a chink in the shutter and fell on Franz's face. He woke up just as the fifth cockadoodledoo resounded.

"I must be dreaming," he thought, sitting up and running both hands through his hair. He yawned, leaped out of bed and ran to open the shutter.

"Lydia!" he shouted. "Come here quick!"

"What?" she said drowsily. "What's the matter?"

"Come here quick, come and look!"

Lydia pushed back her hair and ran barefoot to stand beside him.

"Oh!"

After that one cry of surprise she remained silent.

There in the sunlight a cock, with his scarlet comb erect, strutted proudly through the tall grass. Yesterday's hen

114

walked beside him with a joyous "cluck! cluck! cluck!" and pecked at the ground.

"Oh, Franz!"

"Isn't it splendid? He's come to join her. You can see how happy they are to be here. They won't go away now; they're too glad to have us here. They were left behind, that's clear. They must have been terribly miserable."

"What shall we call them?"

"Caesar," said Franz.

"Why Caesar?"

"I don't know . . . because he looks so arrogant."

"What about the hen then, do we call her Cleopatra?"

They went into fits of laughter at the very idea, and then, as soon as they'd got their breath back, they decided that the name suited her beautifully.

"Oh, how strange it all is!" Lydia said suddenly. "There was just me to begin with on that dreadful night I'll never forget; then there were two of us. And then we found Tao, and that made three. Yesterday evening with the hen, there were four of us. And this morning we're five!"

"Everything comes right in the end," Franz said. He put his arm around her shoulders and hugged her.

"Let's get a move on now. I want to do lots of things today. I've got a plan!"

"Tell me!"

"No, no, I'd rather give you a surprise!"

She looked at him, and saw him laughing in the sun streaming through the window.

"Just as you like, if it makes you happy," she said.

17

It was very cold in spite of the sun, and the atmosphere had changed completely. The air was sharp as a sword blade and had the same incredible purity as the sky above them, so that it was difficult to breathe. The flaming gold and red of the autumn leaves dazzled the eye, and Franz noticed that snow was settling lower on the mountain slopes. He had a sudden idea, and he went down swiftly to the village where he looked very carefully over each one of the deserted houses. Nothing had been left behind, no furniture, no trace of life. Their owners had moved out a long time before. He went into the gardens. There were no fences any more; nothing but a wilderness of stems and weeds and branches run riot together. Everything was still soaked with rain. Franz had to lift his legs high, climbing over fallen trees and pushing back the branches. He was already tall, but the bushes, brilliant with all the colors of autumn, nearly came up to his head.

As he examined everything with great care, he found what he was looking for. There were a few pear trees, bearing small fruit that were quite good to eat, growing against a crumbling wall. Then he found some blackberry bushes and continued his search as though he were looking for buried treasure. He noticed that he was trampling over beds where vegetables had once grown, and crushing underfoot carrot tops growing among weeds, pea and bean plants, and leeks. He felt sure that if he loosened the soil with the spade that stood behind the old wheelbarrow in the shed, he would find potatoes that had sown themselves, growing for no one in particular. These neglected gardens that had gone to seed would be a great help to them. There they could find enough to live on. With the food from these gardens, they could make their small store of provisions last until they were rescued.

They must stop being afraid of this ghostly village. Even though it was deserted, it would be useful to them! The sad village with its ruined houses would become a friendly place.

Franz put some pears in his pocket and gathered a handful of blackberries. He smiled to himself, thinking of Lydia's surprise, and walked briskly back to the house. He was chilled through; his feet, his legs, were soaked; his reddened hands were numb with cold; and his breath hung in clouds about his face.

As he approached the stream, he looked to the right in the direction of their house. Beyond the wood a thin spiral of smoke rose into the blue sky against the mountain, overcoming cold and fear with its promise of life. Lydia was over there, Tao, Caesar and Cleopatra; already a small community was being slowly established, dependent upon one another for well-being and comfort and happiness. When he reached the top of the steps that led to their garden, he stopped in his tracks, astonished to hear a loud barking. A dog came out of the house and bounded towards him, his tail wagging wildly. Lydia ran out too, shouting, "Here! Come here, sir! Don't bite!"

"Where did this dog come from?"

"I've no idea. He arrived just after you'd gone. Caesar was strutting about the garden crowing at the top of his voice, and I was on the doorstep with Tao. Then I heard barking a long way off and not very clear, but it seemed to be answering Caesar. Caesar started crowing again, louder than ever — really, it was just as though he were calling, or sending someone a message. And all the time the barking got nearer and seemed to be answering back. So I was frightened and I took Tao in and closed the door and looked through the window. Caesar went off to the end of the garden, just where the rocks and the pebbles begin, and suddenly I saw this dog. He stopped in front of Caesar, and barked like mad, and Caesar went on crowing — you can imagine the din! Then Caesar came back here, as if he were showing the way. The dog looked up — I think he was looking at the smoke coming out of the chimney — and then he shook himself all over. He came and barked under the window, as if he were talking to Tao and me, then he came to the door and scratched and shook it to ask me to open it for him. I didn't dare. I was afraid he'd jump up at us. But then Caesar and Cleopatra came and stood beside him as though they were saying, 'Open the door for him. He's a friend.' "

"So you opened it?"

"Yes, I opened it. He put his paws on my shoulder. He sneezed and sniffed us and put his muzzle in my hands. He was so sweet I stroked him, and he's followed me about ever since. He seems quite at home in the house."

"It's fantastic!" Franz said. He stroked the dog thoughtfully. It was a mongrel, part Pyrenean mountain dog, part

118

hound. One of those big dogs of no special breed often to be seen on farms. He was dirty and spattered with mud and his coat was wet, but he didn't seem to have starved. He looked with friendly eyes first at Lydia, then at Franz, sneezing for joy each time. He had no collar.

"D'you know," Franz said, speaking his thoughts aloud, "I'm sure our house was lived in long after the village was abandoned. Someone must have stayed behind. An old man, perhaps, who couldn't bear to leave this village. Perhaps he fell ill or became too old to stay on alone. Perhaps he had to go into an almshouse, or maybe he died somewhere on the mountain. We don't know. But one thing's certain — he hasn't been gone long, and his animals are coming back now because they sensed that we're here."

"Look what I've brought you," he added.

"Blackberries!"

"Yes, and some pears."

"Where on earth did you find them?"

"In a neglected garden in the village. There are still some fruit trees and what used to be vegetable patches. It's all overgrown with masses of weed, but I'll go back tomorrow with the gardening tools and wheelbarrow from the shed and clear it. I think I'll find lots of stuff."

He looked around him and went on. "I'll dig over in that corner. It gets all the sun. In the spring I'll plant all the vegetables I can find. I'm sure they'll grow."

"So that when we've eaten all the canned stuff, we'll have vegetables from the garden," Lydia said.

"That's right."

She heaved a deep sigh.

"Well, just for now, come and get warm and have something to eat!"

Inside, the table was set with the coarse bowls and mugs.

Scarlet leaves decorated the bookshelf and the chimney-piece. A good fire blazed under the cooking pot.

Franz went to wash his hands. When he returned, Lydia had closed the door, and the dog, who had come in with them, was quietly waiting near the table. They could hear the happy clucking of Cleopatra in the garden.

"What shall we call the dog?"

"Let's call him . . . Moonflower," she said, when she had given the matter some thought.

"Why?"

"Because he appeared as though he'd fallen out of the moon!"

Franz began to laugh. "It's a funny sort of name. What do you think of it, dog?"

The dog sneezed and wagged his tail to let them understand that he approved.

"Right," said Franz, "you are hereby named Moonflower."

Lydia started laughing too, and they ate their small meal in the highest of spirits.

18

THE DAYS went by. Franz and Lydia put in a lot of work. They had so many plans for the days to come, and so many urgent things to do; the hours flew by so fast, they had no time to feel bored or depressed. Each tried to be gay and bright for the sake of the other, and they both thought up new ways of making their house attractive. It was often exciting, this battle against such great odds. They enjoyed the results they achieved by themselves, and the feeling that their life was becoming not only possible but even pleasant, entirely through their own efforts and resourcefulness.

The keen mountain air had given them huge appetites; they slept soundly, and woke each morning with renewed energy. Tao flourished like a green bay tree, so much so that his jackets and pants were becoming too small for him. Lydia was already planning to make him some clothes from those she had found in the cupboard. He never stopped chattering, or shouting aloud for joy or bursting out with laughter, and he rarely cried. He knew Franz very well, but Lydia better. He would smile at her and stretch out his arms to her; and while he was sleeping, Lydia watched over him with increasing affection.

Once she asked herself whom she liked best, Franz or Tao; then the idea of having to choose between them seemed so dreadful that she made herself think quickly of something else.

Franz had by now dug over the whole of the west side of the terrace that made their garden, for the sun stayed there longer. Lydia had hoed the almost invisible paths and pulled up the weeds. Now it really looked like a garden. Using a chalk stone, they had written OUR HOME in huge letters across the door. That was the name of the house. Moonflower, Caesar and Cleopatra made no attempt to leave. It looked as though they had taken up permanent residence, and looked upon Franz and Lydia as their masters.

Whenever Lydia went down to the stream, Moonflower sat himself down beside the box where Tao slept, and guarded him faithfully, never moving until Lydia came back. Lydia called him "the nanny," and Franz laughed each time he heard her. Moonflower, delighted, sneezed and laughed too, lifting his lip.

Occasionally, shadowy corners of their memory were illumined. One day as he was reading one of their books, Franz said casually to Lydia, "Oh, I remember this — our teacher read it in class."

"What?" said Lydia, sitting bolt upright. "What did you say?"

"I can remember my class distinctly." Franz spoke with an effort. "I can see the others . . . and the teacher reading this book . . . I can see a big window, with a tree showing through the glass — a wet tree . . . it was raining."

"Where, Franz? What town?"

"I don't know."

"What country?"

"I don't know."

"Your name . . . what name did the teacher call you by?"

"I don't know, I can't see anything after the moment of
that reading. Everything's shut down again."

Another day, Lydia began to sing a song to amuse Tao
when suddenly she cried out, "Oh I remember! That song
. . . I can see a room. There's a lot of sun, and white arm-
chairs. Someone putting a record on the phonograph, and
I can remember singing and dancing."

"What else, Lydia?"

"Then, nothing. Just nothing."

These brief recollections saddened them for a while, and
they tried not to think about them. Their various occupa-
tions stopped them brooding.

Generally, Franz went to the observation post every
morning. He had also returned to the Alpine hut and written a letter which explained their presence and showed
where they could be found, leaving it in the center of the
table pinned down by a stone. Lydia busied herself with
the household chores and prepared lunch. In the after-
noons Franz went to the village with the wheelbarrow, and
forked, weeded, dug and cut the undergrowth back. In
doing this he unearthed potatoes and carrots and found
peas all dried up in their pods. He brought them back to
plant in the garden. The thought that they would have
fresh vegetables when winter was over pleased him.

Winter came on quickly. The mountains were never free
from snow; it was icy cold and it grew dark very early.

One afternoon, Lydia went to the observation post with
Franz. She had put Tao into his carry-cot — it was one of
the last times he traveled in it. He had grown so much that

124

she had had to cut one end so that he could stretch out in it. Franz had made a little harness for Moonflower with rope and belt. They put the carry-cot in the packing-case and harnessed the dog to this improvised sledge. It would be the last outing of this kind. An icy wind was blowing that day. The sky was overcast with heavy cloud and there was a feeling of snow on the way.

When they reached the post, they dealt with the signal immediately. The word HELP had completely disappeared and had to be written in again, and to do that they had to light a fire and burn some twigs. They bustled about. The flag threatened to come loose, so Franz climbed up to fasten it securely. Moonflower watched him, and sometimes, barking eagerly, gave a word of advice.

"I wonder if I could get to the Alpine hut tomorrow," Franz said, as he climbed down the flagpole.

"I don't think you'll be able to go out tomorrow. The weather looks so threatening."

"I wanted to have one last look round."

"Yes, but listen!"

A strange sound came from high up in the sky. It was like the muffled droning of a plane. But the sound of a plane is heard in the distance, passes overhead, and fades away again. This sound remained, grew even louder and then after a considerable time, was broken by a prolonged and terrible wailing. The clouds hung low on the mountains hiding the peaks, then lifted again while the snow whirled away from the slopes. The cold grew suddenly more intense.

"What is it, Franz?"

"It's the wind," he said. "Let's get back."

125

19

THE TWO children and the dog set out as quickly as they could go with Moonflower in front pulling the sledge carrying Tao. Moonflower was disturbed. He barked a lot and kept looking back to make sure that his young masters were hurrying. All at once a fierce gust of wind knocked Franz and Lydia off their feet. They struggled to get up, half blinded by the snowstorm whirling about their heads. The gale howled in the treetops, and Moonflower groaned and panted as he dragged his load.

"Franz," Lydia gasped, and she was so breathless she could scarcely speak. "I'm afraid for Tao."

"He's all right," Franz replied, and he too was gasping. "The box is so deep it will shelter him a lot. Keep going, and I'll try to make a hood with one of the blankets."

A moment's lull enabled him to make a sort of awning over the baby with branches and a blanket, and he fastened it down as firmly as he could to the bottom of the box with stones. Tao slept peacefully, unaware of what was going on. Franz quickened his pace and caught up with Lydia just as a twisting column of snow barred their way. Moonflower lay down with his head on the ground.

126

"Lie down, too!" Franz shouted.

The squall passed, and the children and the dog got to their feet, white with heavy snow. At regular intervals snow flurries hurtled against their backs.

The way back seemed much longer. They felt as though they weren't moving at all. The whiteness spread around them, and the familiar countryside looked entirely different, now that the accustomed landmarks were gone.

There at last was the village, already covered with snow. The children were wet through and cold, but they struggled slowly on, sinking into the soft snow that came up above their ankles; the blizzard blinded them with snowflakes, so that they could hardly see a yard in front of them. Fortunately, Moonflower knew his way, and the box he was pulling made a track for them. It was almost dark when they reached the stream. The shining green waters of their first day were gone, together with the feathery leaves through which the sun played hide-and-seek, and the mauve bells that hung gaily on its banks amid the pebbles and the mosses. The stream ran on, but now between two white banks piled with snow. Above the water, the branches of dead trees were interlocked by the wind, and icicles were forming by the waterfall. It was very cold. The children's cold hands were painful, and it felt as though they had no feet, yet were walking on clouds. At last, there at the top of the steps was their little house. Lydia had kept the fire in with logs, so that it would be warm when they returned. At the thought of a fire, their ebbing strength was renewed. Already the house was hemmed in by a drift of snow that covered the lower step. There Caesar and Cleopatra were huddled together. They had left their own shelter, which was the shed at the end of the garden. They must have felt the need to be near the children. Lydia and

127

Franz pushed on, but the gale was blowing harder here than in the village and twice they had to lie flat to avoid snow squalls. Each time Moonflower barked at the house when he got up again. Just for one moment the heavy dark sky opened. For the space of a lightning flash the children saw the highest peak of the mountains towering in majesty against the green sky, its great rock-face loaded with glaciers. Then the clouds drew together and all was dark again.

"Keep your spirits up!" said Franz. "We've just got to get across the garden, whatever happens. Lead the way, Moonflower!"

Holding their heads down, and covering their mouths with their scarves to keep out the icy wind that caught their breath, they sank into the snow, led by the dog, who barked in the lull between two squalls of wind.

It was then that they heard a prolonged lowing, a lowing of distress that sounded strangely through the wind. An animal rushed from behind the house and bounded forward with lowered head and horns well forward. The children, blinded, could hardly see it through the thick snow.

"Franz, what is it?"

"Never mind," Franz said. "We've got to get to the house or we'll be knocked over and buried in the snow."

One last effort, and they had reached the door. The animal came with them as if seeking their protection. The snow had piled up on its back and its head. Franz opened the door, and he and Lydia fell inside, taking caked snow with them. Lydia could hardly get up; she had come to the end of her strength. Franz unharnessed Moonflower and dragged in Tao's box. The wind howled, Moonflower came in, and they were safe.

129

"Franz, Caesar and Cleopatra have come in too," Lydia cried.

"We can't send them outside."

Franz picked up the half-frozen cock and hen and carried them to the fireplace where they shook themselves and plumped up their feathers. Another squall crashed against the door before Franz had time to shut it properly, and just then there was another long bellow of distress. The animal put its soaked muzzle against the window plastered with hardening snow. It seemed to be claiming a place in the house.

"It's a cow!" Franz said.

"Oh, Franz, let her in, we can't leave her out there alone in the blizzard."

They brought her in and she stood with lowered head, frisking her flanks with her tail. She was panting and shaking with the panic that comes upon animals in a violent storm. It was a cow all right; a small cow with curving horns in the form of a lyre.

When the door was securely fastened for the last time, the children and the animals instinctively crowded around the hearth. Lydia felt better and stirred up the fire while Franz threw wood on it. The flames leapt up, and quickly melted the snow so that soon there was almost a lake on the floor. Franz put some water on to boil, and Lydia made tea. They drank it scalding hot while they dried out and Tao's bottle was warming in front of the fire. Tao had suffered least. They lifted him warm and dry from under the hood that Franz had made. He was laughing and full of life, while Franz and Lydia were so exhausted they could hardly speak.

Gradually, the warmth, the tea, and a few rusks made them feel better. Moonflower too had earned a rusk. Caesar and Cleopatra pecked up the crumbs, and the cow lay down and looked at the children with sad, gentle eyes. Outside, the blizzard raged more fiercely as night drew on. Franz lit two candles, closed the wooden shutter, and then wiped up the water spreading by the hearth.

"There are seven of us now," Lydia said at last, looking at the cow as if she were still a little frightened. "Do you think the poor thing came back because she knew we were here, like Caesar and Cleopatra, and Moonflower?"

"Yes, of course. She must have felt the winter and the blizzard coming on and she came back looking for shelter."

"Franz, it would be wonderful if she gave us milk. I get so worried when I think of what we'll do when all the cans of powdered milk are finished. I wouldn't know how to milk her, though."

"We'll try. We've already learned a lot of things. We'll learn that too."

"How shall we feed her?"

"Didn't you say there was hay in the shed? When you took some for Tao's cradle?"

"Yes, there is. But it was just old grass, dry as dry."

"That's what cows feed on in winter, I do know that. Let's hope there's enough of it —"

"There's heaps, and there was more in the store-room. I threw it all outside when I made our bathroom. Franz . . . isn't she sweet, our little cow? She's letting me stroke her . . . But where on earth are the animals going to sleep? There isn't room for all of us in here!"

"The owner must have kept them in what you call the bathroom. It must have been a stable. Anyway, I'll try to get out and find this hay you're talking about. Where did you put it?"

"Quite near. There's a sort of ditch, you know, just by the

131

back of the house. I put it all in that. It's fairly deep, so I don't suppose the hay has blown away."

Franz wrapped one of the blankets around his shoulders.

"I'll come with you," Lydia said. She, too, was swathed in a blanket. The ditch was very near the door of the stable, and though the blizzard still raged Franz was able to collect enough hay to feed the cow for some time.

It was difficult to get her into the "bathroom," for she seemed afraid that they were going to put her outside, and she stayed in front of the fire with her head down, mooing sadly from time to time. Lydia stroked her, to reassure her, and Franz gave her some hay to eat. Then she allowed herself to be led from the room. Caesar and Cleopatra didn't wait to be persuaded. They were familiar with Franz and Lydia, and knew they could be trusted. Moonflower stayed in the main room.

In spite of the frightful tumult outside, Franz and Lydia were able to eat a little. The presence of the animals was cozy and comforting; they didn't feel nearly so alone as they had in their early days. Moonflower watched them. Whenever there was a brief lull, they could hear the cock and hen stirring in the adjoining room, and the cow eating her hay, normal signs of life in this devastating storm. Tao, with no awareness of danger, slept without a care in the world.

Generally, Franz and Lydia went off to bed early to save their candles, but tonight they couldn't bring themselves to leave the fire. For a long time they sat side by side, holding hands and not speaking. Moonflower crouched at their feet. That first sign of the hard winter they must live through was a severe test of their courage. The fire helped to light up the room and set the shadows dancing. Once or twice, when the wind howled even more eerily, or a fall of snow crashed without warning onto the roof, they clasped hands even more tightly.

"Franz!"

"It's nothing," he said, trying to keep his voice steady. "It will all be over tomorrow."

That was the night they began to understand the awful power of the mountains.

20

IT WENT on snowing for hours. The wind died down, but the snowflakes fell unceasingly in a thickening curtain. When Franz opened the door in the morning he was faced with a knee-high wall of snow. He tried to get out through the window, but the snow was still soft and gave way under him. He sank right into it, and had to climb back into the room. Lydia came to stand beside him, and for a long time both looked out through the closed window pane at the dazzling white wilderness that was so bright it hurt their eyes. Nothing was recognizable any more in their garden, or in the pinewood, now entirely covered over. The heavy fall of snow masked the mountains, and there was not a single dark spot on which their eyes could rest. No birds, no sound but the howling of the wind. This was how winter had arrived.

Franz and Lydia didn't allow themselves to be defeated by this new challenge. During the long days when they couldn't go out, Lydia set to work and cut down other clothes to fit Franz and herself, and made some for Tao. She made his big enough and wide enough to wear at the end of the winter. Though his jackets and his cloak were growing very tight, they would do for a few more weeks. It wasn't cold inside the house, for the fire burned well, and Franz had been building the woodpile all through the autumn. While Lydia sewed, he made a sledge from two packing-cases and rope he had brought from the Alpine hut. Regularly he cleaned out the room next to theirs where the animals lived, and buried all the mess in the snow, using the window, since that door was also completely blocked by snow and couldn't be opened. Lydia sewed two blankets together, and Franz filled them with the feathers he emptied from two of the cushions he had brought from the hut to make a sort of eiderdown. They took Tao into bed with them now, so that he would be warmer.

There were no longer any flowers in the house, but it was pleasant all the same, with its shelf of books, its blue pottery jars, and candles on the chimney-piece. Every day Franz added something to make it more comfortable. At the very bottom of the cupboard, so far down that Lydia's arm couldn't reach it, he found another coarse brown blanket. This he hung in front of the door, where it made a thick curtain that prevented any draft from outside. All through the autumn Franz had dug up quantities of potatoes and brought them back, a barrow-load at a time. For the few days they were completely snowbound, they fed Moonflower on them, and he seemed to like this diet. Usually he had to go out hunting game for his meals. Franz and Lydia had tried to milk the cow the day after her arrival, but their first attempt was unsuccessful, and not a drop fell into the bucket Lydia had put ready.

"Perhaps she hasn't got any," Lydia said.

"Yet her udders are all swollen," Franz pointed out. He

135

tried in his turn, but he was no more successful than Lydia.

"Well, there it is, there's nothing we can do about it," he concluded.

But Lydia stayed, disconsolate, the bucket in her hand. When she got up to go, it was as though the cow called her back, mooing at her and turning her head towards the swollen udders, asking her, it seemed, to try again.

That evening they did try again, determined to discover the method, each advising the other, and in the end they did produce a little of the precious liquid.

The cow was infinitely patient. She seemed to understand how difficult it was for them, and how hard they were trying. She watched them with her gentle eyes, occasionally lowing softly to show her affection. They named her Rusty, because of her tawny hide.

Gradually they grew expert, and Lydia particularly learned to milk her as though she'd always known how. They added milk to Moonflower's potatoes, and made it the basis of their own diet. Lydia carefully put away the remaining cans of powdered milk to use when Rusty ran dry.

With the potatoes, Franz had brought back pears and apples. They were not very large, since they had been left to grow wild, but they were good all the same. Lydia found a way of cooking them, and even invented puddings that Franz enjoyed enormously.

"It's such a pity Tao can't have them yet," he said.

The snow stopped when they had been shut in for four days. Franz climbed out through the window and went to fetch hay from the shed, for he thought it would be more sensible to keep as much of it as possible in the stable. Another blizzard might keep them snowbound even longer. There was no means of knowing what lay ahead.

It was icy cold. His shoes, low cut and not very heavy, filled with snow immediately. Climbing the slope of the field was so difficult that he fell once or twice. He was wearing two pairs of trousers, three sweaters, and he had wound a scarf around his head. He made several journeys, loading the fodder into an old basket he found in the shed. Lydia watched him from the window. Moonflower ran backwards and forwards between the shed and the house without a stop, barking joyously.

All at once Franz shouted, "I've found something!"

"What?" Lydia shouted back.

"I've found two sacks, heavy ones."

"Bring them!"

"I'm going to!"

A few moments later Franz reappeared, dragging a huge canvas sack across the snow. Moonflower followed, dragging the second sack, stopping to bark, then taking hold again until they came to the house.

"I only hope they'll go through the window," Lydia said.

"I think they will, but only just."

A great heave and the first sack fell with a thud, raising a lot of dust, and the second followed.

The children quickly unfastened the cord knotted around the first sack. Caesar, Cleopatra, and Moonflower stood by, looking on with an air of curiosity. As soon as the sack was opened, grain poured out onto the floor. Caesar and Cleopatra, with much clucking, fell upon it, beating their wings against each other, determined to get more than a fair share, and in a trice had gobbled it all up.

"What is it, Franz?"

"I'm wondering whether it's buckwheat . . . I saw some stems of it in a field full of weeds. A field that must have been cultivated once."

"What's it used for, Franz? Can you make bread with it? But it would have to be ground."

"Oh yes, it would have to be ground, and we've nothing to do it with. No, we'd better keep it to feed Caesar and Cleopatra. Just look what a feast they've had!"

Caesar and Cleopatra, who for four days had put up with a meager diet, pecking at the cow's fodder, picking up crumbs from the table and potato peelings, were now clamoring loudly around the sack. Lydia gave them another handful of grain, and they fought for it under Moonflower's scornful eyes.

"What's in the other sack, Franz?"

"Let's open it, it feels like sand."

It was difficult to get it open, for the cord was tight and they didn't want to cut it in case it might be useful. The most ordinary thing could prove precious.

It was not sand, but a sort of flour, dark in color.

"Is it buckwheat flour, Franz?"

"Perhaps — I don't know."

"Do you think we could use it?"

"We must be careful not to poison ourselves . . . I know what we can do," he said, after a moment's thought. "We'll make some porridge, and give it to Moonflower. If it's not edible, he won't eat it."

"Are you sure? What if it made him sick?"

"It won't. Animals know much better than we do. Don't worry, he won't make a mistake."

Lydia made her porridge with some of Rusty's milk, and gave it to the dog, who swallowed it in a flash, and licked his chops after it, wagging his tail.

"You see, it must be buckwheat," said Franz. "We'll wait till tomorrow before we eat any ourselves, to make quite certain. But I'm sure he won't be sick."

The following morning, Moonflower was in the very best of health, and Lydia decided to make bread. The supply of rusks was running low, and she planned to put them aside with the powdered milk.

She made a very thick paste, beat it and turned it, slapping it again and again with a wooden spoon.

"You think that's the way to make bread?" Franz asked, watching her with a somewhat skeptical eye.

139

"That's how you make biscuits, I know. So why not bread? It'll be a kind of bread anyway."

Then they realized that though they had a fire, they had no oven.

"I'll make you one," said Franz. "It's the only thing to do, and it'll be very useful."

They put aside the rounded shapes Lydia had made, and as soon as breakfast was over, Franz started to make the oven from a large can that had contained butter. That evening they set it up for the first time over a glowing fire, put the rolls inside, and waited.

"But they almost look like real rolls," Franz said when Lydia drew them out.

Lydia looked at the dismal objects and began to laugh. Franz laughed with her when he saw she wasn't upset. "I'll do better the next time," she said. "You just wait and see." But they ate them anyhow and decided they were absolutely delicious and a lovely change from rusks. With the rolls they had potatoes, milk and canned ham, and as far as they were concerned, that meal was the finest banquet in the world.

21

So THE problem of bread was solved, as well as that of milk, for Rusty's supply was abundant. Lydia put it in a pan each evening, and in the morning it was covered with thick cream. It suddenly occurred to her to skim the milk with a spoon and keep the cream in a jar. Then, when she had enough, she began to beat it with a wooden spoon.

"What are you doing, Lydia?"

"Making butter," she answered confidently.

"You know how to make butter?"

"I know you beat cream to make it, so I'm trying, that's all. We'll see whether it works."

She had to go on beating for a long time. Franz took over whenever she felt tired. It looked as though they would be disappointed, but Lydia held firm.

"Let's go on a bit longer. It would be so wonderful if we managed it. I remember," she went on, and her voice sounded odd — "Oh yes, I remember . . . I was in the country, and Marie was there . . . Marie had a blue apron. She beat the cream for ages, in a special pot, I know she did. And then I tasted the butter, and it was awfully good."

"Oh! wie gerne würde ich mich an etwas erinnern können!" said Franz, his eyes staring as if trying to pierce the shadow covering his past. Lydia looked at him desperately.

"Franz, you're doing it again, I can't understand what you're saying!"

"Was? aber ich sag Dir doch . . ."

"Franz, you're not speaking the same way I do! You're talking gibberish. Franz!"

"Dieselbe Sprache . . ." he said, like a sleepwalker.

And he put his hand to his head, just as he had done the first time.

"What is it?"

"Now, yes, you said, 'What is it?' and I understood you. Franz, what's the matter? Are you ill?"

"No, I'm not ill. I know quite well what I said . . . I believe that when you don't understand me, it's because I'm speaking in another language."

"Another language? What language, Franz?"

"I don't know . . . but it's a different one from yours all right, since you don't speak it. There's nothing to be scared about, Lydia. I suppose I just change words without noticing, because I don't see any difference . . . But I'm perfectly well. Don't worry about it. . . . Oh!" he shouted. "Lydia, the butter — we've done it! Look!"

At the bottom of the jar a compact white lump was forming in a sort of greenish liquid. Lydia cried out in delight and forgot her worries.

"Beat it a little longer and harder," she said. "I knew we'd do it!"

Franz went on beating and, when at last they were sure the lump wouldn't grow any larger, Lydia shaped it into a pat with the spoon and put it in a dish. They tasted it.

"It's good, but a bit sour," Franz said. "Suppose we rinse it in water?"

They threw a whole jug of water over the little pat of butter, and when they tasted it again, it was delicious.

The problem of butter was solved.

Deep winter spread its vast white sea around them. A frightening silence, almost as frightening as the blizzard itself, reigned over the countryside embedded in a cottonwool nest of snow. Occasionally the majestic peaks gleamed through a rift in the sky, so dazzling it was impossible to stare at them for long. Here and there a diamond column stood rigid against a sparkling rock face, a waterfall, frozen stiff in its falling by the mortal cold.

Franz tried out his sledge and found that it went well. He harnessed it to Moonflower, and the dog enjoyed pulling it as they toured the garden. Lydia had cut down for them the two cloaks she had found in the cupboard and had even managed to make a small one for Tao out of the pieces left over.

One sunny day they all set out for a walk. The steps leading to the stream were completely buried in snow and formed a smooth slope. They lifted Moonflower on to the sledge and tobogganed down, Franz directing it with the ropes fixed to the steering. At breakneck speed they shot down to the stream, now frozen into a mirror, and drew up at the beginning of the village with a dizzying sideways spin that nearly unseated them all. Moonflower barked like mad. Lydia screamed and laughed, and so did Tao. The sound of shouting and laughter broke into the silence of the grim mountains and echoed around the frozen landscape.

They harnessed Moonflower as soon as they were on the level, and he set off like an arrow. Sometimes Franz ran

alongside to help him. In this way they came to their observation post. The tree had held firm and the wooden
signpost too, but the flag had disappeared and the words
on the board had gone. They dug into the snow with the
spade and pick that Franz had brought with him until they
came to stones. Then they made a blazing fire that warmed
them up nicely, while Franz charred some twigs and wrote
HELP once more on the signpost, with an arrow showing
the way.

"You never know, someone may come. You can't be sure —"

"When winter's over," Lydia said, "we'll put up another flag."

They ate some bread and chocolate, and returned home in a brilliant sunset and a deep silence broken only by the muffled sound of snow dripping from the trees, or the snap of a branch broken under the hoar frost.

Thousands of crystalline snowflakes glittered like jewels in the bushes, and to Franz and Lydia it seemed as though they were treading a carpet patterned with deep, rich colors. The rows of pines glowed with a purple light for a brief moment, then the sun disappeared behind a peak, and by the time they came back to the house, they left nothing behind them but gigantic violet shadows.

22

ONE MORNING Franz, who had gone out to cut more branches for the woodpile, penetrated the forest just beyond the stream on the other side of the village. They had been there only once before, the day they had tried to get away and had climbed up to the col, but then they had only skirted the fringes of the forest. Franz was enchanted by the majesty of the crystal dome above his head. Every tree looked transparent with fringes of hoar frost dangling from it in slender needles sparkling in the sunlight. The path he was following came suddenly to an end in a jumble of rock and then there was a sheer drop to the valley. He cut more wood, adding it to the bundle on his back, and was about to turn back when he saw the paws of an animal sticking up out of the snow. He dug into the snow and uncovered the body of an animal that he did not recognize. It must have been killed by the fall of a branch or a stone, for its skull was crushed. The snow had kept it in a state of good preservation, and it had a short-haired gray coat and a bushy tail. Franz thought that the fur, if he were able to treat it, would be very useful to them. Both he and Lydia suffered terribly with their feet and hands. Their light shoes, rapidly wearing out, and their gloves that had grown too small, offered no protection. He wondered, if he gave his mind to it, whether he might not be able to make shoes and mittens out of this fur.

He remembered — for memories were gradually coming back into his mind — he remembered reading books about the knights of old, which explained how huntsmen skinned and then dressed the skins of the animals they hunted. Just recently he had discovered how to tan a hide in one of the books brought back from the Alpine hut.

"I won't say anything to Lydia," he decided. "I'll give her a surprise. I'll come back here this afternoon with the big knife we've got at home, and I'll try it out all on my own. She'll be tremendously impressed." He buried the animal in the snow again, stuck three small twigs over the place to mark it, and returned with his bundle of wood, very excited.

His plan was successful. He skinned the animal without too much damage to the fur, remembering the instructions he had read. It was a nasty job, and several times he felt he would have to give up. His head was dizzy and he felt sick. But he forced himself to go on, thinking of Lydia's hands, her fingers that sometimes bled, and her feet so frozen when she came back from their expeditions that it took a long time to bring them back to life. It hurt her so much she had to fight not to cry. He so badly wanted to be able to make gloves and shoes for her and for himself. Tao, too, for he would soon be walking and then he would need shoes.

Franz buried what remained of the animal, rubbed the raw skin with snow and then stretched it out as flat as possible, holding it down with stones. The weather was clear and dry, and tomorrow he would come back again.

147

Franz spent several days in this way. He set out every morning, saying he was going to get wood, but instead he went to the forest to watch over his skin. Then came the time when he brought it home, swilled it with water in the big jug in the shed, and finally put it to soak by the fireplace in an old bucket.

"What's that, Franz?"

"Oh, just the skin of an animal I found in the snow."

"What are you going to do with it? Make a rug or something?"

"I don't know — I'll see."

One afternoon they lit the candles earlier than usual for the heavy sky was dark. Franz fetched his tools from the cupboard in the store-room, so that he could work on the skin. He had just brought them to the fire when the steady humming sound they had heard once before when the blizzard came, began in the distance, grew louder, swelled deafeningly, and burst upon their little house.

"It's the hurricane," said Franz. "Here it comes again."

"It's stronger than last time."

"Maybe, but at least today we're at home."

"Thank goodness," said Lydia. "What a difference it makes!"

She went into the stable to reassure the animals, who were disturbed by storms, stroking them, and giving hay to Rusty and grain to Caesar and Cleopatra. As she was lifting the hay, she felt something hard and warm.

"Franz!"

She ran through the door.

"Eggs! Cleopatra has laid some eggs!"

She put them on the table and they both looked at them, astounded.

Just then a real tornado shook the walls, cracking the

148

trees like a whiplash, and sending a load of hard snow against the window like a bomb exploding. They paid hardly any attention to it. They were laughing as they looked at each other, and then at the beautiful smooth eggs, just faintly tinged with pink.

"Thank you, Cleopatra!" said Lydia.

"You must give her some more grain to reward her," Franz suggested.

Cleopatra had already gone to roost, perched on a beam of the sloping roof, modestly unaware of having done anything remarkable. She did, however, come off her perch to get her additional ration. Caesar immediately stole half of it from her.

"What a fine dinner we're going to have," Lydia said, coming back to Franz. "We'll be able to keep our cans in reserve now, and when Tao needs more than milk and rusks he can have eggs too."

While Lydia settled herself by the fire with Tao on her knees, Franz lifted the animal skin which had been soaking for some days, and set about scraping and stretching it.

"What are you doing, Franz?"

"I'm experimenting with something."

"What?"

"I'm trying to use this skin to make shoes. We'll soon be going barefoot."

"What a good idea! My old ones are hurting me already, and they're all in holes. But do you think you'll be able to?"

"It shows how to do it in one of our books, but of course I don't know whether this will work. I don't have all the things I need."

When he had scraped the skin, he coated it all over with fat he had melted down in the autumn when they had roasted a dead bird of prey he'd found on the way to the look-out post. They had used the feathers to make an eider-down for Tao's cradle, Moonflower had been only too glad to eat the meat, and they had kept the fat.

Once the skin was well greased, Franz hung it in the stable, near the animals. Then he washed his hands and came back to Lydia.

"I'll leave it to dry now," he said.

Outside, the howling of the blizzard and the force of the gales increased. Once more the children felt afraid. Even Tao began to cry and wanted to be put down. He already enjoyed trying to stand upright, but now when Lydia put him on his feet, he didn't want to stay there, but started crying again. She had to pick him up and rock him gently to soothe him. He was heavy for her small arms, and jigged about so much that she found it difficult to hold him.

"I'm going to give you a surprise," Franz said. He took from the cupboard a sort of short stick, scraped clean and almost smooth, pierced with holes.

"What is it?"

"A reed pipe I've made."

"What's a reed pipe, Franz?"

"A sort of flute. You'll see."

He sat down beside her and blew a note on the pipe.

"Oh, it's wonderful! Where did you learn how to do that?"

"I don't know . . . I don't know. It's all hidden in the dark, like all the rest . . . But when I found this hollow stick in the shed, I thought of making this, and when I blew on it, the tunes came back to me."

"Try it, Franz. I want to hear."

So Franz played an old tune, a sort of folk song, with an odd little rhythm.

"Oh, Franz, that was so pretty! Do you know any more?"

150

"Did you like it?" he said, as though he were pleased. "Yes, I do know some others, and I'm going to play them all to you!"

Now the blizzard could howl as much as it liked, and the pines groan with the same sinister voice. Franz went on playing, and Tao was lulled to sleep. Lydia and Moonflower listened to the music full of sweetness and sunlight and joy. Lydia put Tao in his cradle and began to dance. They forgot their terror, and they entertained themselves until it was time for supper.

"Franz, if you can find another stick, will you make me a pipe?"

"Would you like one?"

"Oh yes!"

"I'll go and look where I found it. There's sure to be another one."

"We haven't once thought of the storm outside!"

"And a good thing, too!" he said.

Lydia gave Tao his supper. When he had been put to bed, she and Franz sat down and enjoyed a fine meal made from Cleopatra's eggs.

Outside it was as though the whole mountain range were howling. This blizzard was far worse than the other, but the children were so filled with music that they fell asleep at once, light-hearted and profoundly happy.

23

AND THE winter went by.

Franz had had some success in using the fur to make rough shoes with wooden soles, and clumsy mittens that kept their hands very warm indeed. At first they had difficulty walking in their new shoes, but they soon grew used to them. Whenever the weather was fine enough, they set out on the sledge which stood up well to the strain. They would go to the look-out post, or to the stream, or walk a little way along the path that led to the col.

They enjoyed wonderful days when the sky was a transparent blue, the whole countryside sparkling like diamonds, and the air crystal clear.

Franz had made a pipe for Lydia. In the evenings, when the candles were lit, he taught her how to play it. Lydia was musical and she learned quickly. In a few days she could play an accompaniment to the tunes Franz drew from his pipe. One day she made up some verses about the snow and the stream, and a little lost lamb, and she sang them while Franz played. He thought the song beautiful.

So every evening passed like a dream, whatever the

weather was like. All day long they struggled hard for their bare existence, but as soon as evening came, it was time for enjoyment. They would spend some time reading, and occasionally one of them read aloud to the other; afterwards they made music. Moonflower would sit down to listen in a very dignified manner while Caesar and Cleopatra rushed in and perched on the chimney-piece. One evening, Rusty herself arrived, mooing sadly, as though to reproach them for leaving her alone. She stood chewing a mouthful of hay, quite at ease, and whisking her tail as a sign of contentment. From that day on, it was tacitly agreed that all the animals should listen to the concert.

They never made a sound, but listened in a respectful silence. One evening when Lydia made a mistake, Moonflower put back his ears. When she repeated the wrong note a few moments later, he barked. On another occasion, when she had been dancing, Rusty, who had watched her attentively with her large eyes, began to moo loudly; then Moonflower barked, Cleopatra woke, went "Cluck! Cluck! Cluck!" . . . and Caesar, carried away by the general enthusiasm, gave voice to a resounding "Cockadoodledoo" even though it was completely dark.

"They're shouting 'Encore'," Franz yelled in fits of laughter.

Lydia began dancing again, and they immediately fell silent.

Outside, the weather went its own way, and the terrible winter drew to its end.

With the coming of good weather, Lydia, Franz and Tao began taking walks again. One day, when they had gone on beyond the observation post, they came to the bluff with its sheer drop down to the valley. They heard a sound of light galloping, muffled by the snow.

154

"Oh! What funny goats!" Lydia called out. She pointed up to them.

Three graceful animals with long slender legs were leaping from rock to rock above their heads. They disappeared as fast as lightning.

"They're not goats; I don't know what they are!"

"They're beautiful. We frightened them. I wish they'd come back. It's more fun when there are animals around."

They often went in the direction of the Alpine hut in the hope that some rock climbers might have passed there. Lydia and Tao waited while Franz climbed up to the very door. But they never saw anyone.

Each time they came back to their house with the same delight, as they saw it half-buried beneath a thick layer of snow, crowned with smoke from the chimney.

One evening, when they were neither reading nor enjoying their music, but just dreaming in the firelit room without bothering to light the candles, Lydia said, "Franz, I want you to talk to me again the way you do when I can't understand what you're saying."

"But, Lydia, you're always frightened when I do that."

"No. Tonight I want you to, because now I know it's just another language. Speak to me that way, Franz."

"But . . . it's difficult to do," he said. "Usually I don't even think of it."

Franz waited a moment, as if he were collecting his thoughts, then he looked at her.

"*Von ganzem Herzen liebe ich dich*, Lydia," he said.

"*Von ganzem Herzen liebe ich dich*," she repeated with an effort. "What did you say, Franz?"

"I said I'm very fond of you, Lydia."

"Oh! What a nice thing to say!" She was pleased.

The following morning, when they woke, Franz got up

155

to open the shutter and get the fire going as he did every morning. When he came back, Lydia held out both hands to him.

"*Von ganzem Herzen liebe ich dich,* Franz."

She said it very quickly, as though she had been rehearsing it.

"How did you remember it?" he said, astonished.

"That's my secret," she said. "Franz, I want you to teach me a little every day to speak like you. And when we leave here I'll know —"

"I'd like to, Lydia. I'll say things to you every day and you can repeat them after me if you'd like to."

"Oh yes, I would . . . I don't like to think you can speak in a way I can't understand," she said.

24

IT SEEMED one morning that winter was suddenly over. There was still much snow, to be sure, but there was a mildness in the air. Flocks of birds flew by, coming from the col and following the course of the valley. Every day the sun rose a little higher, felt a little warmer, and shone on the frozen landscape and the house for a little longer. They saw the frozen covering of the shrubs slowly disappear and the trees begin to rain heavy drops of melted snow while the weather remained calm. Whenever they went out, snow dropped from the branches on to their faces and since it was always unexpected, they would shriek with laughter. The thick white covering over the earth grew gradually thinner, and holes appeared in it here and there. Franz and Lydia were delighted to see the first primroses raising their heads to the sun; and then one day, though they didn't know how it happened, and couldn't believe it possible, there was nothing left of all that snow but a few patches in shaded corners. They could see the color of the soil again and the young green grass starred with a thousand wild flowers. The stream began to sing once more and the mauve flowers leaned over the water again.

Now they were happily settled and their surroundings were familiar to them, Franz and Lydia grew to love the harsh landscape that could show a gentler face. The neglected gardens in the village were also filled with flowers; and in their own little garden the rye and the vegetables Franz had planted put out strong young shoots.

Franz made a sort of lobster pot from dried rye stems, for he had seen fish farther down the stream near the forest, and it seemed a good idea to go and fish there. He set out one morning eager to lift the pot he had sunk the day before. He came back proudly with three fish. Lydia boiled them and they feasted on them.

Then Lydia thought of braiding the rye stems tightly into slender cords. She fixed the cords over a piece of wood, as though on a small loom, and wove them to make a kind of sandal. Obviously, they wouldn't last long, but she could soon make others, for there were plenty of dried stems in the shed by the field.

Rusty came out of the stable and was put in the meadow; she expressed her delight in the noisiest way possible. Caesar and Cleopatra began scratching in the garden, and returned to roost in the shed; the "bathroom," cleaned and aired, went back to its former function.

The days lengthened, and it grew steadily warmer at midday. Lydia looked like a boy, dressed in trousers and a shirt with the sleeves rolled up. Only her hair, hanging around her shoulders in a golden mass gave away the fact that she was a girl. She wanted to cut her hair off to make it easier to manage but Franz had been so against it that she had given up the idea.

Instead she cut Franz's hair, and Tao's, by a very simple method. She just put a basin on their heads and chopped

off everything that showed below the rim. This gave them a hairstyle that was rather attractive, though a little odd. Tao's hair was blacker than ever, and his skin smooth and pale. He was growing more and more Chinese and he had a way of looking at Lydia, his slanting eyes gleaming with fun and the corners of his mouth turned up, that she found irresistible.

He was walking now, holding on to Franz's hand or Lydia's, or by himself, while they held out their arms to catch him if he fell. His teeth had come through without any trouble; he was small, but strong and healthy. The mountain air had kept them all healthy, and none of them had been sick a single day. Franz had grown; his trousers were too short, and so were his shirtsleeves. He just rolled them up, and left his collar undone. Hardened by the intense winter, neither of them suffered from the cold any more.

Tao began to talk. He said "Fan" and "Eda" with an earnest expression. Franz and Lydia laughed at him, and he laughed too, showing off. He was a happy child, and very good. Moonflower adored him, watching over him all the time, and stopped him getting out of his cradle on his own. Lydia could always leave Moonflower on guard with an easy mind.

When the days grew really long, the three children sat in the doorway every evening, and rested in the silence of the solitude they now took for granted. Their practiced ears were aware of the subtlest sounds, the snap and fall of a dead branch, the rattle of a pebble falling down a slope, the distant song of a waterfall. Of all these, they loved best the sound of the bell they had found on a shelf in the shed, and tied around Rusty's neck where it tinkled with every movement.

160

Sometimes Lydia worried because their clothes were wearing out; because they would soon be without sugar, even though they used it as sparingly as possible to make it last; because their candles would hardly see them through another winter.

"Something must happen soon," she said to herself. "It can't go on like this."

But she feared even more the thought of leaving everything that was now their life; and when she realized that their return to those places they couldn't even remember would probably separate them, she felt as though she were torn in two. Sometimes they discussed it, and then Franz did his best to reassure her.

"We still have just enough for another winter. The summer after that we'll be bigger and stronger. Tao won't be so helpless, we've got Moonflower and Rusty, and we can try to get back. If we go much farther than we did before, we're bound to come to a real village."

"But suppose they find us and separate us, Franz?"

"Yes, I'm sure that's what would happen," he said. "And I couldn't bear it either."

25

THEY WENT often to the observation post, and they kept the signpost in good repair. They had fastened another piece of canvas to the pole to serve as a flag. And then it was midsummer. They recognized the look of the country-side. It was exactly as they had seen it on that first day.

One evening Franz said, "I'd like to suggest something I think we ought to do."

His voice was serious, and so was his face.

"I'm listening," Lydia said, equally grave.

"Tomorrow I want us to pick the most beautiful flowers in the garden and take them to the church. You said it was dirty, so we'll give it a good spring-cleaning and make it as beautiful as our house."

"I know what you mean," she said at once. "We'll go tomorrow."

When Franz woke up the next morning, he saw that Lydia was already up, and had everything ready for break-fast. She wasn't in the room, but Tao was also up and already dressed.

"Where are you?" Franz shouted from the window.

"Picking flowers," she replied from the garden. He went

to join her, and they soon had an armful each, to which Lydia added wild roses from the bushes around the door. It was a day of gold and crystal, the air sharp and pure, but it looked as though the sun would warm the atmosphere as soon as it had mounted higher in the sky.

Lydia gazed up at the mountain peaks, shielding her eyes with her hand.

"It's going to be very hot. I shall tie something over my head, and Tao's too."

As soon as breakfast was over, Franz brought out the sledge. Lydia lifted Tao into it, and he almost disappeared among the armfuls of flowers. Then they set out, taking with them a broom, a brush, some rags, and two jugs that they filled at the stream as they passed it.

Moonflower seemed to be enjoying himself the most. He leaped about, barked at the top of his voice and set all the echoes going, thrashed the air with his tail, and jumped right over Tao's head as he sat in the sledge. The more Franz and Lydia laughed, the more he played the fool. Franz harnessed him as soon as they were at the foot of the stairway while Moonflower watched him with his fine deepset eyes, and occasionally licked his hand gently.

At last, with Moonflower pulling the sledge, Tao chuckling happily and playing with the flowers, and Franz and Lydia following on behind with the jugs filled at the stream, they came to the church.

It seemed to be expecting them, a small low-roofed building with overhanging eaves to protect it from heavy snowfalls during the winter. More panes in the windows were broken, and a large crack had appeared in the bell tower. At the end of the nave, by the porch, water had come in and hadn't yet dried out. The wind had blown down the little confessional.

163

Franz looked around, admiring the ceiling sown with stars, and the angel about to fly away with his great wing sweeping along the curve of what had once been a pointed arch.

"It must have been a fine church once, but how neglected it is now!"

He put Tao by a chair, and tied him to it with his belt. "Quick, let's get to work!"

At once all the things that were so damaged, so damp, so forlorn, and so cold took on new life. The warmth of the morning sun streamed in as the day lengthened.

Dirt, dust and cobwebs disappeared beneath the onslaught of broom and brush and duster. Lydia went busily from time to time to shake out her duster, while Franz swept away fallen plaster, broken masonry reduced to powder, loose stucco and dead leaves.

Lydia, sitting on the altar steps, cut the flowers and arranged them in the vases. She had freed Tao, who was now playing on the floor on his blanket. Moonflower had fallen asleep in the sun outside the porch.

They managed to set up the confessional again after a fashion, and wedged it with two chairs. Franz mounted the steps that led into the pulpit, and leaned on his elbows to look at the body of the church.

"Does it look pretty, Franz?"

"Yes, it does," he said. "From up here it's even better than from below. You must come and see."

"I will in a minute. I'm just finishing the flowers."

She got up and put the vases on the altar one by one, climbing on a chair because she wasn't quite tall enough.

"Do you want any help?"

"Thanks, but I've nearly finished. Do they look all right like this?"

"Bring the left one forward a little."

164

"There?"

"No, towards the middle."

"Here?"

"Yes, perfect. Come and see, quickly!"

Lydia gathered up the stems and the leaves that were strewn over the steps.

"I'm coming."

She gave one last flick with the broom, and came to join him. They both admired their work for a long time, leaning on their elbows.

"Oh, Franz, it's absolutely beautiful. Just as if there were going to be a wedding!"

They fell silent, overcome by a sense of veneration. The scent of roses hung in the air, and the wide-eyed marguerites bowed gracefully before the little crumbling doors of the tabernacle.

"Franz —" Lydia said at last, "— don't you think it must be a year since that dreadful night, when everything was so blurred and so extraordinary?"

"Yes," he replied. "About a year. The sun was in the same place when we woke up that morning, and the garden was filled with the same flowers as these."

"Franz — why not make today our birthday — today, when we happened to think of coming to this poor church and decorating it for a festival?"

"Why not? We can say we're celebrating three birthdays all at once. I'll make a calendar tonight so that we can count all our days from today."

She went on. "Think of all the things that have happened since last year! We met each other, we found the stream, the house, the Alpine hut; then the hen came, the cock, Moonflower, and Rusty . . . don't you think, Franz, we should say thank you?"

166

"I think you're right, Lydia. Let's stand up and give thanks. And then we'll go back to the stream."

They stood for a few minutes, upright, very grave, and silent. Then they gathered up their cleaning things, Lydia folded Tao's blanket, Franz took the child in his arms and they walked out slowly. Seeing them, Moonflower burst into a frenzied barking, leaping up first at one, and then at the other.

"This is a special occasion, Moonflower," Lydia told him as she harnessed him to the sledge. "Today is our birthday."

Moonflower barked even louder. Before they set out, they took a last look along the nave to the flower-bedecked altar. Then Franz noticed a rope with two large knots hanging onto the right of the porch.

"What's that, Franz?"

"It must be the bell. Oh, Lydia — shall I ring it?"

"What a wonderful idea! Ring it, Franz, oh do, as this is a special day. I'll go outside and listen."

Franz pulled on the rope several times with all his strength, then ran after Lydia. The bell started ringing as soon as the tugging of the rope reached it, and a joyous peal rang out in the sunlight that bathed the street and the mountainside. Looking up, overjoyed, the three children and the dog listened with the same wonder as if it had happened out of the blue, one Easter day.

As the peal died down, they set off for home. The bell was still ringing spasmodically, and the vibration echoed through the mountains.

The peaks sparkled against the dazzling blue of the sky, and the heat haze shimmered in the sun. The children put away the things they had taken with them as soon as they got home, then picked up their reed pipes and went down to the stream. It was as welcoming as it had been the first

167

day they had seen it, cool, clear and filled with music, edged with moss and garlanded with mauve flowers and green leaves. All three children, with their faithful dog, spent the day they had decided to call their birthday beside the stream. They sang, and played all the tunes they knew on their pipes. They made up others.

26

So THE summer went by. For Lydia and Franz, gathering in the harvest they had sown was the greatest excitement of all. Nearly everything they planted had come up successfully, and their potatoes were much bigger and better than those in the deserted gardens. Those gardens, however, continued to yield treasures. By working there when he could, Franz had brought one of them back into cultivation; he had pruned the fruit trees growing there and could see now the excellent results he had achieved. He found it fascinating to experiment, for he had nothing to lose, since the gardens belonged to nobody. There was no one to scold if things went wrong, and it was exciting when things went right. Both the apples and the pears were much finer than in the previous year, and there was a good crop.

That particular garden, which they called "the orchard," became the goal of some of their walks. They went to sit there, taking a lunch with them; sometimes they saw the graceful izards, the wild mountain goats of the Pyrenees, that Lydia had described as "a funny sort of goat," silhouetted on the peaks surrounding them.

One evening towards the end of the summer when they were resting in front of their house, they heard the tinkling of bells not far off, but it wasn't the sound of Rusty's bell. They saw two sheep coming towards them, timid but determined; one of them looked very fat. The other began to baa, almost as though it were explaining something. The fat sheep seemed to be exhausted. Lydia went slowly towards them, and began to stroke them. Then, still baaing, the first sheep went around to the back of the house and stopped in front of the door to the stable, as though it wanted to go inside, the fat sheep following close behind.

"Let them in, Franz, they're such darlings!"

"They'll make it dirty."

"Never mind. Just for tonight . . ."

So Franz gave in.

The next morning the fat sheep had two lambs suckling at her side.

"It's a ewe," said Franz, and Lydia was enchanted. It was wonderful luck, for Rusty was beginning to give less milk; they kept it all for Tao, first taking off as much cream as possible to make butter.

Tao was, of course, now eating eggs and vegetables, and even fish. Every day Lydia took some milk from the ewe to use for cooking, and she and Franz drank it, and found it good.

Just like Moonflower, Caesar and Cleopatra, and Rusty, the sheep remained, and seemed delighted to stay. In the spring Cleopatra had sat on her eggs and hatched six chicks, round fluffy balls like powder-puffs that had grown into six fine chickens. When winter announced its sudden arrival once more with a blizzard, the door of OUR HOME closed protectively on seventeen healthy living beings.

And it all began again. . . .

170

It was at the end of that hard winter, and eagles swooped over the garden on menacing wings, that Franz heard, one evening, a strange droning sound. He lifted his head suddenly, his face flooded with scarlet, and strained to hear.

"Is it another blizzard, Franz?"

"No. Listen . . . can you hear?"

"What is it, Franz?"

"A plane!" He could hardly breathe the word. "A plane!"

They opened the door, paying no heed to the cold. Moonflower howled as though he had gone mad. Just then they heard the sound of an explosion, the dark sky was lit up as if by a gigantic lightning flash, and a great glow spread in the sky.

"It's over by the look-out post," Lydia said.

"Put your cloak on quickly. I'll get the sledge. We must hurry!"

"Franz, the snow's melting already."

"So what?"

"And what about Tao? Franz!"

"Bring him; we must have Moonflower."

"But it's dark."

"It's all right. We know the way."

They set out.

The snow was still hard under the trees, and they went at a good pace until they reached the village. After that it was more difficult, but Moonflower nearly killed himself pulling the sledge, groaning in his frenzy to reach the plane, and sometimes barking loudly.

"You see, he's taking us to the look-out," Franz said.

As they drew nearer, they realized that the fire was beyond the look-out, on the slope of another mountain with a sheer drop into the valley.

"Shall we go back, Franz?"

Moonflower had no intention of going back. He pulled the sledge as if he knew exactly what he was doing, nosing at the snow all the time.

All at once he howled so loudly that he made the children jump, and grew so agitated that Franz unharnessed him. He streaked off like an arrow.

"I'll go after him," Franz said. "You stay here with the baby." They disappeared into the darkness.

Lydia stayed alone, shivering more from shock than from cold. They had stopped the sledge just by the dense thicket where they had found Tao, a tiny creature with hardly any life left in him. Now here he was asleep, wrapped snugly in his cloak, his head on her knees already growing heavy — that small baby had grown into a healthy child . . . now nearly two years old. Memories of that dreadful night brought a lump to her throat, for once more that same red glow lit up the sky and made the dark mass of the tall mountains seem nearer. She wondered what had happened this time, and what they would discover.

Time passed slowly; then she saw Franz and Moonflower silhouetted against the glowing sky. They stopped frequently, for they were dragging something that seemed to be very heavy. When they drew near, Lydia saw that it was the body of a man.

They reached the sledge at last. Lydia tried to help Franz to revive the man. He was wearing the outfit of a parachutist, but his parachute must have been torn off, or perhaps he had struggled clear of it before he lost consciousness.

"He must have crashed on a rock and banged his head,"

172

Franz said. "We found him at the foot of it; he must have rolled down."

"Do you think he's dead, Franz?"

"I think he's breathing, but I can't listen to his heart through all these clothes."

They managed at last, with considerable effort, to unfasten some of his thick clothing. Franz slapped his face and his hands, and raised and lowered his arms. He gradually regained consciousness, groaned, and muttered a few words that the children did not understand. Franz and Lydia spoke to him, but he didn't understand them either.

He raised himself up a little, looked around, and was clearly astonished to see the two children and a dog. Then he began to shake, and his teeth chattered.

"We must get him to the house as quickly as possible," Lydia said. "He'll die here."

He didn't seem to understand. Then Lydia suddenly thought of speaking to him in Franz's language, that she could now speak fairly well. He showed signs of understanding, but they had to repeat everything very slowly. At last he answered them, in the same language, certainly not his own, but familiar to him.

Lydia made a place for him on the sledge, while Franz helped him to his feet.

"Lean on me. Don't be afraid to; I'm very strong."

"Oh, he's bleeding!" Lydia said.

Blood was streaming down his face.

"It's from my head," he said.

The children made him as comfortable as they could with the blankets, then Lydia slid in beside him with Tao on her lap. Franz harnessed himself side by side with Moonflower.

Their journey back was long and difficult. The snow was thawing, and from time to time the sledge sank into it. The wounded man found it painful, and Tao, half-awake, cried a little. But it was still more difficult to get up the incline from the wood to the house. Franz had to hack out footholds on the glassy slope with his pick. When the sledge had been hauled up, Lydia helped the young man to climb, for he could hardly keep on his feet; then Franz went down again to fetch Tao, who had been left near the stream, fast asleep, rolled in a blanket.

"Where am I?" the wounded man asked when Lydia opened the door of the house. "What country is this?"

"This is our home," said Lydia.

With a great effort, he took off his equipment. Lydia carefully bathed his face, and cut the hair away from the wound as closely as she could. Then she cleaned it, tore up a towel, and used it as a bandage.

It was more difficult than it had been to bandage Franz's leg. The wound looked deep, and it was bleeding heavily, but Lydia seemed to have a gift for these things, and she made a good job of it. The young man was looking around in amazement.

"Where are the others?" he said.

"What others?" asked Franz.

"The grown-ups."

"There aren't any."

"But what are you doing here?"

"We're waiting."

With infinite care, they helped him on to the bed, where they made him lie flat. Lydia settled him as comfortably as she could and made him drink some tea.

He seemed to relax and closed his eyes, no longer trying to understand.

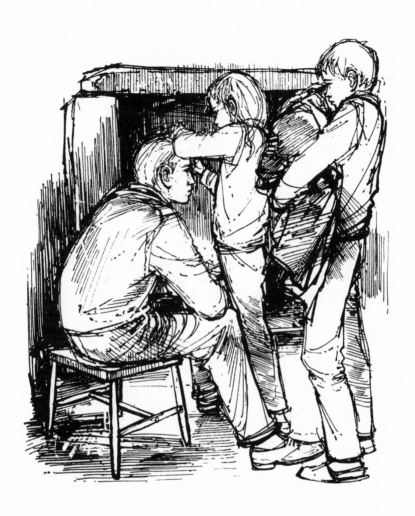

The two children slept on the floor in front of the fire, on a quickly arranged bed of hay covered with a blanket.

That evening a message had been picked up by an air base in Norway: "Engine on fire. France. Central Pyrenees. Néouvielle Peak. Balaïtous. Bailing out. Stop."

27

From one base to another, the alarm was passed, a reconnaissance plane was sent out, and a team of guides from Barèges set out for the mountains. The weather was overcast, and low clouds masked the outcrop where the deserted village slept secretly.

Snow had begun to fall again. The first day of the search brought no success. On the morning of the second day, however, a rift in the clouds enabled the reconnaissance plane to make out the wreckage of the Norwegian machine, wedged between two rocks on the slope where it had burnt out. A message was relayed to Pau. A helicopter went up, hovered over the valley and came down between two peaks in search of a landing place. The rescue parties on the slopes, one making for the Néouvielle Peak, the other for the Balaïtous, were using the helicopter as guide. It was in this same area, two years before, that a plane had been lost without a trace.

The helicopter landed and men stepped out onto the children's observation post. There was no trace of the first burnt-out plane, but the flagpole was still standing at the look-out post, and the white flag, only recently renewed, was flapping in the swirling mist. The men went up to examine the pole, and saw the signpost, where Franz had, just a little while before, carved the word HELP into the wooden board.

The men had a word together, and then set off in the direction of the arrow.

Meanwhile, the Norwegian pilot was installed in the little house, bowed under its winter wrappings, but snug and friendly all the same. Franz had drawn some pictures, and fastened them to the walls, together with a portrait of Lydia and one of Tao. Lydia had made a carpet of braided stems, like their sandals.

Franz, Lydia, and the young man had chatted like old friends, sitting by the hearth in front of the fire, using Franz's language, which the pilot could understand. He was amazed at the story they told him, and at the ease with which the two children changed from one language to the other, their efforts to go on learning, the courage with which they had overcome difficulties, and the life they had created for themselves.

The lunch and dinner with which he was served added to his surprise and still left him unprepared for the concert they gave for him that evening, when Franz played his pipe and Lydia danced.

He had already expressed his deep gratitude to Moon-flower, who had found him in the snow. But now they introduced Rusty to him, and Caesar and Cleopatra with their six chicks, and the four sheep, who, warm and comfortable in their shed, spent their days peacefully awaiting the spring.

He was so delighted with it all that he forgot his injuries,

177

and the message he had transmitted just before he bailed out.

So it was that on the second day, just as they were about to have a meal, the rescue party, led by the smoke rising into the gray sky, tapped on the window pane and were amazed to hear peals of laughter coming from the house.

The three children, pale and completely bewildered by the situation, watched the men armed with ropes and skis and ice-axes invade their home.

Franz had told their story. Now his forehead glistened with sweat and his heart was beating fast, for one of the men who seemed to be the leader, wanted to take them away at once in the helicopter.

"That's impossible!" said Lydia, and she burst into tears.

"We're very grateful to you, sir," Franz said, "but truly, we can't come away just like that. We haven't got anything ready. After all, we must do a certain amount of packing, and leave everything tidy. It's true we haven't very much . . ." he added and his voice shook, "but . . ."

"And there are the animals," Lydia said. "We can't leave the animals. If they can't come with us, then I want to stay here." And once again tears ran down her face. She couldn't hold them back.

"Please forgive us," Franz said. "We are most terribly grateful to you for having come to look for us. But if you don't mind, could you just take this gentleman with you today? He's hurt, so he should be taken care of. If you could possibly come back in a few days, we could put our affairs in order, and get everything ready . . . and then . . . we can come away . . . so long as our animals can come too."

"The weather may be against us in a few days' time,"

the man objected. "We might not be able to land. It looks as though there'll be another blizzard any time now."

"All right," Franz said. "Then we'll just wait for you to come back in the spring. We've already spent one winter here, and most of this one . . ."

The simple men from the mountains were deeply moved. Some of them had families of their own, and were very much against leaving the three children behind, alone. They couldn't understand how deeply the children now identified themselves with the wild countryside, at once so harsh and so gentle. They did at last agree to go without them, but only on condition that Franz and Lydia clear everything up quickly so that they could be collected as soon as possible.

"What about the animals?" said Lydia.

They promised her that Moonflower, Caesar, Cleopatra and the chicks should travel with them in the helicopter, and that a sledge should be brought for Rusty and the sheep.

The Norwegian pilot hugged all three of them with deep affection. He didn't know how to thank them.

"That's all right," Franz said. "We couldn't have done anything else."

The men disappeared across the garden and into the darkness, for night had come. The light from their lanterns dwindled among the pines, and their voices faded in the distance. Then the great silence came again.

Franz and Lydia stood side by side at the window, their arms around each other's shoulders. They still had not spoken when, after a long while, they heard the roar of the helicopter passing over their heads on its way out.

Then they looked at each other and Lydia began to cry again.

179

Four hours later, radio stations throughout the world sent out the news. It was dinner-time in the dining-room of an apartment in Paris where a man and a woman were sitting at table. They seemed sad. Each was making an attempt to talk, to cheer the other.

"Shall I turn the radio off?" the young woman asked. "Does it bother you?"

"Oh heavens, no, not if you'd like it on."

"It's the news . . . we'll turn it off afterwards."

"Just as you like."

And it was like the flash of a thunderbolt:

"Three children have been found in a deserted village on an outcrop in the Barèges upper valley, between the Néouvielle Peak and the Balaïtous. The children, aged about two, fourteen, and fifteen, have been living in this uninhabited region of the mountains for more than eighteen months. The two oldest are suffering from a partial amnesia and can remember only their Christian names, which are Lydia and Franz."

A description of the physical appearance of the three children followed.

The husband and wife stared at each other. The same impulse brought them both to their feet.

"Did you hear?" she said at last, in a voice that could scarcely make itself heard.

"Yes!" he cried out, and his voice broke. "Lydia!"

One hour later, the headlights of their car were piercing the darkness on the Chartres road, traveling towards Pau.

28

THE FOLLOWING day the blizzard did return, less violent than in midwinter, but nevertheless bringing plenty of wind and snow with it. Anxious glances were lifted from Barèges to the upper valley. The rescue party, ready to set out at once, could do nothing but wait.

The little house lost in the clouds was filled with sadness. It is only when we have to give things up that we discover how much they mean to us, and Franz and Lydia, young as they were, were learning that hard truth. They would never have believed how much they loved their darling house, the garden they had brought into being again, the orchard over in the deserted village, that even now was preparing its springtime magic under a blanket of snow. The mountains, so vast and majestic, so primitive but so beautiful, always changing according to the time of day — the church, and the stream, their first friend.

They couldn't bear to leave it all, never to see it again; never to hear again the gay sound of Rusty's bell tinkling on a summer evening, never to be waked again by Caesar's bold cockadoodledoo as the sun rose; never to sit around the hearth, all three of them, on a winter's night, to read, or play the pipes, surrounded by the animals.

They began to get ready to leave, and they had no heart to talk. The animals must be in perfect condition when they were fetched; the stable left spotlessly clean and neat, and the house exactly as they had found it.

Franz took down the drawings from the walls, while Lydia brought out the clothes in which they had arrived. They were far too small, and it was impossible to get into them. Lydia folded them carefully in one of the boxes brought back from the Alpine hut. Then she packed all the woolies and leggings, together with the carrying cloaks, into the bag that belonged to Tao, for he had outgrown them long before they were worn out.

Franz returned the books that had entertained and taught them to the hut, but they were in tears when they let them go. But they both kept their pipes. Franz wrote a letter which he left in a conspicuous spot on the table in the hut:

"Please forgive us for having taken food and other things, but we had to or we would have died. We know that we must pay our debt and we will do so as soon as we possibly can." He signed it "Franz," since he did not know his other name.

And then they were ready. They wore the rough clothes that were so wide and oddly-shaped. Lydia still wore the medallion, bearing her Christian name, around her neck.

They spent a sad night in the dead house, where only the fire was alive. Moonflower seemed to sense what was going on, and stayed stretched out on the floor, his head on his paws, following his young masters only with his eyes, sighing deeply.

But it was a week before a huge sledge arrived, drawn by three mules, and driven by two men. They had come to fetch the animals. A few moments later the children heard the roar of the helicopter. They brought Rusty and the sheep out of the stable; the animals looked at the children with anxious eyes that seemed to be asking what was happening. Franz and Lydia hugged them all.

"We're coming too," Lydia told them. "We'll meet you again down there."

As soon as the sledge started moving, Rusty mooed so loudly that the mountain echoed with the sound of it, and the sheep began to baa with all their might. The sledge disappeared behind the wood.

Franz closed the door of the house very carefully. The pilot heaped their odd luggage into the helicopter, and then put the chickens in, their feet tied together. Caesar and Cleopatra settled down with a few protesting murmurs. Moonflower wouldn't go in until the children did. Lydia entered first, holding Tao by the hand. Franz came to sit beside her, and then Moonflower, barking furiously, hurled himself inside as though afraid of being left behind. The rotor-blades turned. Huddled together in their odd-looking hooded capes, the children watched the gleaming peaks of the mountains rush by and their eyes filled with tears.

"Goodbye, dear stream! Goodbye, dear house! Goodbye, dear church! Goodbye, all our flowers!" Lydia cried.

"Bye!" called Tao, waving his hand.

"We'll come back," Franz said solemnly. "I promise you we will."

"Mummy!"

183

Lydia recognized her at once, as though something within her had torn apart, the moment she saw her in the distance when they reached that unknown town.

"Mummy!"

And suddenly the cloud over her mind disappeared. She remembered everything. She had been traveling alone, by plane, from the country in which they had been living, and she had been put in charge of an air hostess. It was for the holidays — she was on her way to her grandmother, who lived near Paris, and her parents were going to join her there a few weeks later. She remembered . . . the plane . . . Daddy and Mummy, below, waving their handkerchiefs; and then the journey . . . the bunks at night . . . she had fallen asleep . . . and then, nothing.

"Mummy! Daddy! Mummy!"

She was in their arms now, laughing and crying, she didn't know what she was doing or what she was saying. Franz and Tao stood a little apart, hand in hand. There was no one for them.

Once again the headlights of the car were piercing the darkness, this time making for Paris. In the back, three children and the dog crouched at their feet were falling asleep, their heads nodded.

"Are we dreaming, Franz?"

"I don't know any more," he said.

Lydia's parents had taken Franz and Tao to stay with them until their families should claim them. Moonflower too, naturally. They had also arranged transport for the animals. Rusty, the four sheep, Caesar, Cleopatra, and the chickens would follow by train and go to their country house near Paris. They could be visited every Sunday and all through the holidays.

Then in the morning they reached Paris, misty blue at

the beginning of a fine March day. Through the windows of the car, Franz looked at the barges gliding along the Seine. He gripped Lydia's hand.

"I'm beginning to remember now. I can see my school ...I was a boarder...Grandfather...my parents are dead...Grandfather is an artist. He painted in Montmartre and sold his pictures to foreigners...I am Austrian ...I live with him."

"Why were you in the plane, Franz?"

"Wait...Yes, I know. I went away for a month...with friends of my grandfather...they were traveling on business...Grandfather couldn't look after me just then, so they took me with them. I was on my way back. Do you think, Madame," he asked Lydia's mother, "that Grandfather knows?"

"I expect so, though I can't really tell you. We heard the news on the radio by pure chance, and we set off at once as fast as we could go."

They had arrived. They got out of the car, and Lydia recognized everything with a sort of wonder. An elderly man was waiting for them in the apartment, striding up and down the hall impatiently. He had come from Vienna, the city to which he had returned in his great grief. He had learned the name and address of Lydia's parents from the radio, and had come for news. The porter had told him that the children were expected at any moment.

"Grandfather! Grandfather!"

Now Franz was laughing and crying too.

There was still no one for Tao, but he was too young to realize it. For him, Lydia was his mother.

An hour later reporters arrived, and Franz and Lydia were interviewed. They did not know what to say, and didn't understand why there was so much fuss. Yes, they were up there, lost, so they made out as best they could . . . nothing extraordinary about it.

They found that they were being offered a reward, they were asked what they would like . . . Why? . . . They had saved Tao . . . and the pilot? . . . Well, so what? Nothing odd about that — how could they have left them to die? They really must say what they wanted? There was something, but it was probably quite impossible . . .

"We've already thought about it," Franz said. "We want to go back there every year. We left our gardens, and the stream, and we want to see them again. But above all we want . . ." His voice grew surer. "We would like a big house to be built beside ours, to take in sick children who haven't a home, and those who have no parents. The air up there is wonderful, they could get well, and they'd be happy, like we were."

"It must be for all kinds of children," Lydia said. "Not just for French ones, for we came from three different countries, and we loved each other like brothers and sister. It must be for any lost children in the world."

"The village could be rebuilt," said Franz. "There are enough houses up there to take a lot of children, and we could go to see them every year."

The children's wish was made known and a fund was set up voluntarily. The village would be rebuilt, and a road suitable for cars, to replace the rough path that had caused them so much trouble.

Franz and Lydia would go back every summer.

Franz's grandfather returned to live in Paris, for he did not have the heart to separate Franz and Lydia.

No one claimed Tao. The passenger list showed that a Chinese woman had embarked on the plane with her baby.

187

But no one had come forward since the disaster took place. So Lydia's parents were allowed to keep little Tao with them.

At the country house near Paris, the animals were happy, and did not seem to miss their mountains. Franz, Lydia, Tao and Moonflower went to see them every week.

It was not long before the first building began to rise in the village. It would perhaps become a town, where unhappy children from all over the world could be cared for, cured and made happy again, simply because one evening three other children, with compassionate hearts, fell out of the sky up there.

ANN A. Flowers, Patricia Lord, and Betsy Groban edited the introductory material in this book, which was phototypeset on a Mergenthaler 606-CRT typesetter in Primer and Primer Italic typefaces by Trade Composition of Springfield, MA. This book was printed and bound by Braun-Brumfield, Inc. of Ann Arbor, Michigan.

Gregg Press
Children's Literature Series
Ann A. Flowers and
Patricia Lord, *Editors*

When Jays Fly to Bárbmo by Margaret Balderson. New Introduction by Anne Izard.

Cautionary Tales by Hilaire Belloc. New Introduction by Sally Holmes Holtze.

The Hurdy-Gurdy Man by Margery Williams Bianco. New Introduction by Mary M. Burns.

Nurse Matilda by Christianna Brand. New Introduction by Sally Holmes Holtze.

Azor and the Blue-Eyed Cow by Maude Crowley. New Introduction by Eunice Blake Bohanon.

The Village That Slept by Monique Peyrouton de Ladebat. New Introduction by Charlotte A. Gallant.

Squirrel Hotel by William Pène du Bois. New Introduction by Paul Heins.

The Boy Jones by Patricia Gordon. New Introduction by Lois Winkel.

The Little White Horse by Elizabeth Goudge. New Introduction by Kate M. Flanagan.